THE
BICYCLIST'S
GUIDE TO THE
GALAXY

FEMINIST, FANTASTICAL
TALES OF BOOKS AND BIKES

EDITED BY

ELLY BLUE

ELLY BLUE PUBLISHING,
AN IMPRINT OF MICROCOSM PUBLISHING
PORTLAND, OR + CLEVELAND, OH

THE BICYCLIST'S GUIDE TO THE GALAXY
FEMINIST, FANTASTICAL TALES OF BOOKS AND BIKES

Edited by Elly Blue

All content © its creators, 2023

Final editorial content © Elly Blue, 2023

This edition © Elly Blue Publishing, an imprint of Microcosm Publishing, 2023

First printing, December 5, 2023

All work remains the property of the original creators.

ISBN 9781648411861

This is Microcosm #735

Cover art by Gerta Egy
Design by Joe Biel

Copy editing by Esa Grigsby

Elly Blue Publishing, an imprint of Microcosm Publishing

2752 N Williams Ave

Portland, OR 97227

This is Bikes in Space Volume 10

For more volumes visit BikesInSpace.com

For more feminist bicycle books and zines visit TakingTheLane.com

Did you know that you can buy our books directly from us at sliding scale rates? Support a small, independent publisher and pay less than Amazon's price at www.Microcosm.Pub

To join the ranks of high-class stores that feature Microcosm titles, talk to your local rep: In the U.S. **COMO** (Atlantic), **ABRAHAM** (Midwest), **IMPRINT** (Pacific), **TURNAROUND** (Europe), **UTP/MANDA** (Canada), **NEW SOUTH** (Australia/New Zealand), **GPG** in Asia, Africa, India, Latin America, and other countries, and **FAIRE** and **EMERALD** in the gift market.

Global labor conditions are bad, and our roots in industrial Cleveland in the '70s and '80s made us appreciate the need to treat workers right. Therefore, our books are MADE IN THE USA.

MICROCOSM · PUBLISHING

ABOUT THE PUBLISHER

ELLY BLUE PUBLISHING *was founded in 2010 to focus on feminist fiction and nonfiction about bicycling. In 2015, Elly Blue Publishing merged to become an imprint of Microcosm Publishing that is still fully managed by Elly Blue.*

MICROCOSM PUBLISHING is Portland's most diversified publishing house and distributor, with a focus on the colorful, authentic, and empowering. Our books and zines have put your power in your hands since 1996, equipping readers to make positive changes in their lives and in the world around them. Microcosm emphasizes skill-building, showing hidden histories, and fostering creativity through challenging conventional publishing wisdom with books and bookettes about DIY skills, food, bicycling, gender, self-care, and social justice. What was once a distro and record label started by Joe Biel in a drafty bedroom was determined to be *Publishers Weekly*'s fastest-growing publisher of 2022 and #3 in 2023, and is now among the oldest independent publishing houses in Portland, OR, and Cleveland, OH. We are a politically moderate, centrist publisher in a world that has inched to the right for the past 80 years.

[TABLE OF CONTENTS]

INTRODUCTION

*A*s I write this, the U.S. is having a particularly dystopian moment. The pendulum is swinging back hard from the catharsis of 2020. Abortion bans are spreading. Racist violence is on the rise. The pandemic isn't ending, but we're acting like it is. Book bans are starting to be eclipsed in the news by state legislation that criminalizes trans people's very existence, and there are plenty of foreboding signs about what's next in this poorly conceived, depressing story.

I was planning to write this introduction about the crossover of books and bikes in my career, and how this volume of stories combines the two topics so deliciously. But now I'm tracking the pendulum of the news, and the joyfully goofy nature of this project—still running strong, ten years later, on the impulsive spark of "what if we did a feminist bike zine but with sci-fi stories"—just doesn't seem to be reading the room.

Even so, looking back at other spates of bad news in my life and in the news, the biggest lesson of Bad Political Shit is the power of the impulse to resist, the intensity of communities coming together to spark something new and different. First you have to imagine it, then you have to fight like hell to make it happen, and books can fuel both of those parts. We need both the books that are going to be banned, the ones that serve a desperate need, and the ones that allow a momentary escape into creativity, into "what if," into a more inclusive or just radically different reality. If I've learned anything from my years as a bike activist, it's that we won't do the work, or at least not well and not for the long term, if we can't also ride together, whooping exuberantly, through the streets to the dance party.

And, for what it's worth, banning a book is one of the best ways to get it in front of as many readers as possible. It's been wondrous to watch librarians, teachers, booksellers, publishers, authors, and a glorious plethora of incensed readers put their formidable intelligence, networks, and organizational skills to work distributing life-changing books like *Gender Queer* and *All Boys Aren't Blue* to thousands of young people who need them—and who possibly never would have found them if they hadn't been banned.

Despite having enough queer and trans characters to make a Republican state legislator's eyes bleed, it's unlikely this book will ever gain the widespread audience needed to be banned, but you never know. There are some heartening stories in here of bicycle tourists resisting fascism, a young child outsmarting the faerie court, a lefty political figure escaping an oppressive alien blockade, sporty middle-aged lesbians rebuilding their lives after a pandemic, and the slowest rider on the team uncovering the key to everyone's desires.

And that's what it's all about. This volume covers the emotional gamut, from happy to sad, whimsical to intense, personal anger to political rage. Books are a topic bound to inspire, and when I put out the call for submissions for feminist bicycle science fiction and fantasy stories with a theme of books, I received so many excellent stories that I accepted enough to fill two volumes. At a loss as to how to split the stories up, I ended up putting the ten longest pieces in this volume. The second one comes out in the spring and has fifteen shorter stories and an emotional range all its own, from hilarious to thoughtful to epic.

I hope you love all the stories in both books. I hope nobody tries to take a book you love away from you, or your human rights, or your own wild and weird story. If they try, please know that there's a community out there willing to fight like hell for you.

Elly Blue
Portland, Oregon
June 2023

THE RIDE FOR THE CITY
✑ Kathleen Jowitt ✑

Half an hour to wait. Well, at least it's not raining. She could get a coffee, get out of the biting East Anglian wind. She *could*. She has the money, just about. She shouldn't, though.

Well, then, what is she going to do with half an hour? She considers riding around the block a few times—it would keep her warm, wouldn't it?—but it's not going to be much fun in rush hour, and besides, there's a whole empty bike stand there, and who knows whether it'll still be empty when she gets back? No. Lock the bike up, and then decide what to do next.

She's bending over to loop the cable through her back wheel when a square of bright red catches her eye. A book. In the basket of the next bike along.

It can't hurt to look, she tells herself.

The Fallow Fields. A thriller, by the look of it. *It's happened before. It could happen again.* . . . Shadowy figures, red on red.

Well, that's one way to fill half an hour.

She glances around. She feels a bit awkward picking it up— it's not her bike, it's not her book—but it's not as if she's actually taking it away. If the owner returns, she can give it back. In the meantime . . .

The owner does come back. Carly doesn't notice until she hears that little exclamation of surprise and looks up. A student. Got to be. One of the rich ones, though. She's beautifully dressed, with a tailored blazer over perfectly fitted jeans and turquoise suede brogues. And she's just plain beautiful, with flawless brown skin and thick, shiny dark hair. Carly feels rather as if she's been caught pocketing the spoons at Buckingham Palace.

There's no point pretending she isn't reading this woman's book. "I'm sorry," she says. "Can't resist a book."

Any trace of hostility dissolves in a wry grin. "My own fault. I shouldn't have left it there. I'm glad you were enjoying it, anyway."

Carly holds it out, but the student shakes her head. "Finish it. I haven't started it yet."

She wants to protest. But she also wants to find out what happens. "That's very nice of you. How can I get it back to you?"

The student grins. "Why not put it back where you found it? I lock my bike up here every day."

It seems like a bit of an unreliable way of doing it, but it's not her book they're proposing to leave lying around. She takes it home and finishes it in relative comfort. Next day, she'll go back, look for the bike, get the book out, put it in the basket.

That's all very well, but it feels a bit . . . rude. Abrupt.

She doesn't have a lot of books at home, and she's reluctant to part with most of them. Of the rest, three are too trashy to admit to, and one was so bad she couldn't finish it. But she feels like she's obliged to return the favour. In the end, she selects *Cold Comfort Farm*. She saw a copy in the hospice charity shop the other day. If she loses this one, it won't be the end of the world.

She thinks hard about whether to put something with it. Is that going to be a bit weird? But then this whole thing's a bit weird, isn't it? In the end, she writes: *Thank you. Really enjoyed reading this. This is one of my favorites. Carly K.*

Her book reappears with something called *Come Listen to Me* and a note replying: *That was hilarious! How have I never read it before? Hope you like this one. Soraya x*

Soraya. Now she can put a name to the face. Now they're all square.

The book is rather daunting: nominated for all sorts of awards and written in a weird, broken style. But after a while she stops trying to follow the confusing punctuation choices and just goes with the flow. She reciprocates with a collection of ghost stories.

If the Roald Dahl one scares you, she writes, *beware of the M.R. James.*

The next time, they don't need a note. Soraya's there, locking up her bike. When she sees Carly, she grins and reaches into her bag. "I thought I could do with something less challenging. I begin the term with very lofty intentions of reading all this intellectual stuff, and I get less and less ambitious the harder my studies get." She hands Carly an Agatha Christie book. "I'm not going to tell you a thing about it. Sometimes it's just nice to be dazzled by someone else's brilliance."

Carly, who has never thought of herself as having enough brilliance to need to be dazzled by anyone else's, raises her eyebrows and takes the book.

She devours it in a weekend.

She's glad to be able to hand it back in person, too.

"I know they always say it's the person you least expect, but that's a whole different level."

Soraya grins. "Yes, she manages to stop you suspecting some people at all, doesn't she?"

They swap *Summer Fling* and *The Mystery of the Peaks*, and Carly locks up her bike and goes off to her appointment.

She's almost disappointed, a few days later, to see Soraya's bike there and no book in the basket. She tells herself off: it's not like the woman's under any obligation.

Then she sees it. On the ground. It's got a cloud-wreathed mountain, a dragon, and a lady warrior, all of which seem to be defying the laws of gravity in their own particular ways. The title's written in mock-runic capital letters. *The Sorcerer's Crown*.

Poor Soraya, she thinks, her course must be getting really heavy going.

She picks up the book.

It's a gorgeous clear evening, with a bit of warmth left in the sunshine, and she doesn't have to be anywhere for another hour at least. She sits down, gets herself comfortable against the arm of the bench, and opens the book.

It delivers on the promises of the cover. It's a somewhat formulaic tale of a stable boy who turns out to be the lost heir to the kingdom. With the aid of a magical mentor, a small and reasonably competent band of traveling companions, and sheer force of will on the part of the author, he brings his enchanted scepter to the usurped city and claims his rightful crown. It's compelling reading nonetheless, and the minutes and the chapters slip past without Carly noticing, until she and the story reach the city gates—which are immediately flung open to welcome the new king.

"But how did they know it was him?" she begins to say, out loud, but is silenced by a sharp jolt in her solar plexus.

It's as if the ground moves underneath her. She flings out a hand to steady herself, grabs something, but it doesn't help: she's still lurching. *Falling*.

Everything goes dark. There's just the air rushing past her face and whistling in her ears, and a strange whirring sound that she can't quite place. It's coming from somewhere beyond her left hand, which is still gripping . . . what? It's round and metal, and she'd thought at first it was part of the bench, but it can't be, because that was all wood. Then she realises: it's part of a bicycle. Presumably Soraya's. She holds on tighter.

She lands with a bump. The bike lands on top of her.

"Ouch!" It's a hard floor. She blinks, looks around. There isn't much to see. A small room, pathetically illuminated by a single, tiny, high-up slit of a window. A blanket. Something in the corner she doesn't want to look at too closely.

And a familiar face.

"Oh, thank goodness." Soraya looks almost as if she's ready to hug her.

"How long have you been here?"

"About a month, I think." She shakes her head. "No, that can't be possible."

Carly says, helplessly, "It's six o'clock in Cambridge."

Soraya nods. "What day?"

"Tuesday."

"Then I can only have been here about three hours."

"And where's here?"

Soraya glances pointedly around the bare walls and nods at the heap of bones in the corner. "What's it look like to you?"

"We're in the book." She doesn't bother making it a question.

"This is the dungeon where our hero got locked up at the end of Part Two."

"Right. So do you think anyone's going to bribe the jailer to find us a change of clothes and let us out, the way they do for him?"

"They haven't so far. Let's assume they won't, and get thinking."

They think.

"You know what kind of book this is," Carly says at last.

"Mm-hmm. Are you saying we should be using our feminine wiles to persuade our captors to let us out?"

Carly grimaces. "Couldn't have put it better myself."

"Ugh. Maybe we should wait another half an hour just to make sure nobody's going to bribe the jailer for us."

"I suppose it wouldn't hurt. It'll give us time to work out what we're actually going to do when we get out of here, anyway."

"When. I like that *when*. So much better than *if*."

"I guess I should ask: Where had you got to when you got here? Where in the story, I mean?"

Soraya raises her eyebrows. "Oh, it was nearly the end. It was the bit in the palace when the loyal general was explaining how the resistance had spiked the city walls. So to speak."

"You got further than I did, then."

"You mean you caught on quicker." Soraya disarms the comment with a swift grin.

"You think . . . ?"

"Well, let's make sure. What happened *to you* when . . . ?"

"When I got to the city gates? I wondered how on earth the defenders had known that this was the chosen one, and bang! here I was."

"Same. I mean, I was wondering the same thing, at a different point. And, as you say, bang."

But Carly's suddenly uncertain. "We're right, aren't we? It just couldn't have worked. There was no way for anyone in the city to prepare for the hero's party. They couldn't have known."

"So it was a plot hole of such an intense gravitational pull that it sucked the reader in?"

Carly laughs. "Seems like."

"It makes no sense."

"I think we have to make it make sense."

"Do you think that'll get us out again?"

She isn't at all confident. "Got any better ideas?"

Soraya pulls a face. "I guess it's worth a try." She sits down on the floor. "So, come on, what's got to happen?"

"The rightful heir's got to get to the palace, obviously."

"With the magic scepter."

"Yes, because it's his birthright."

"But he takes care of all that himself. I wonder if we've been anywhere else in the book. Maybe you're the mysterious lady in the vision in chapter . . . five, was it?"

"I'm not wearing *that*," Soraya says.

Then Carly hears something. A young man's voice. She clutches Soraya's arm. "Listen!"

"My friends, don't be downhearted!"

"It's him!" Soraya breathes. "It's the heir!"

Carly nods.

The voice continues: *"We are few, but our cause is a true one and the people will be with us, will rise up for us. . . ."*

Soraya's smiling almost despite herself. Carly listens carefully, in case she missed something when she was reading this. But it doesn't tell them very much. That, Carly supposes, was really the problem in the first place. There's a lot about destiny, and not very much at all in the way of detail. Still, they listen to the whole speech, all the way through to its last line: *"When once we find our way out of this place, we ride for the city."*

"Well," Soraya says, under the cover of ragged cheering from the heir's companions. "There we are. Now we know. Officially, I mean. And now that we know, we can take the news. And then the city can be ready to receive them."

"You think that's what we have to do?"

"That's how we make it make sense."

"And we have . . ." Carly frowns, thinking back over what she read. "About a day, I reckon. They don't make camp, or sleep, or anything, on the way, do they?"

"They accept a bowl of soup from the woman in the village who turns out to be the heir's old nurse and tells him the password for getting the secret documents out of the treasury."

"Oh yes, of course they do. But that can't delay them for more than half an hour or so."

"Yes, and it's sunset when they reach the city."

They look at each other. "We've got to get away before they do."

"And to get away, we've got to get out. Hang on a moment." Soraya tries the door. "Oh, for goodness' sake. I am such a *lemon*."

"What?" But Carly knows.

Soraya pushes the door open. "Nobody bothered locking *us* in."

"Come on, then. Let's go."

"Aren't you forgetting something?"

Carly looks around the cell. "Oh. Yes. Sorry."

Soraya turns back and picks up the bike. The least Carly can do is to hold the door open.

They tiptoe down the long corridor, the gentle clicking of the freewheel sounding horribly loud in the silence. A rattle of metal sounds louder still. Keys. They glance at each other and duck into an empty cell. Footsteps are approaching. Two people, Carly thinks. They're getting closer and closer and closer.

Soraya's fingers are digging into her arm. "Come on," she hisses when the footsteps have passed. "There's just a chance they didn't lock the main door after them."

The owners of the footsteps have disappeared around a corner. Carly and Soraya run for it, Soraya just about keeping quiet when she runs a pedal into her own leg. But at last they're out of the door, into the morning sunshine. Nobody's looking for them. Nobody knew they were there. That's something. But they've got a long way to go.

Soraya mounts the bike. "Go on," she says. "Get on the rack."

"Things you *don't* want to hear when you're stuck in a fantasy book," Carly observes, but she straddles the rack over the back wheel. She wraps her hands around the seat post. "It's been a very long time since I've done this."

"Hold on tight!" And Soraya pushes off.

"The roads are surprisingly good," she remarks in a yell after a mile or so.

"I wouldn't complain, if I were you."

"What? I'm not complaining. I'm just wondering whether the author . . . or if he . . ."

"What?" Carly can't hear.

Soraya slows to a stop. Carly gets a foot down just in time. "I was saying," Soraya said, "that either the author didn't think about it, or there's a good plot-related reason for there to be a nice fast road."

"My guess is option one. If he'd thought about things we wouldn't be here."

Soraya laughs, and presses on.

After about an hour, they swap over. Pedaling is harder work than balancing on the back, obviously, but Carly finds she doesn't have to think so hard as she did when she was the passenger, and it's actually quite a nice change. Soraya's right about the road. Tarmac would be too much to ask for, but the small stones it's paved with are unexpectedly smooth. The hero doesn't come this way; he joins the high road only at the very end of his journey.

In the meantime, the road is long and featureless, and it's a tedious ride to the city. Nevertheless, neither of them really wants to be stuck in this world, so they keep on riding, taking it in turns to pedal or to cling onto the back.

"Hang on," Carly says after a while, "what's that? There, on the horizon?"

Soraya brings the bike to a stop so that she can look properly. "I think we might be getting somewhere."

Carly nods. "Let's keep going."

After about another five minutes, the road plunges abruptly into a forest.

"This is where the party joins the high road," Soraya says. "I wonder if we're still ahead of them."

"We've got to be. They take a stupid long way round. But don't they follow a little stream down to the road? I could really do with a drink of water."

The stream is only a minute's ride further on.

"Do you think it's safe to drink?" Soraya asks.

"We have to hope so."

Soraya doesn't argue. And the taste of that sweet, fresh water is very welcome indeed after a hard ride. They take the opportunity to have a rest, too, sharing a chocolate bar from Carly's pocket and a flapjack from Soraya's. "On the edge of the wood," Carly says, "there's an apple tree where they stop and eat the fruit. It should be safe for us, too."

"We must be working on fantasy logic," Soraya says. "We ought to be far more hungry than this."

"Don't knock it."

The forest is pleasant to ride through: cool and shady, murmuring with birdsong and the rustle of leaves. Refreshed by the snack and the drink, they enjoy the interlude.

"Say what you like about the usurping ruler," says Soraya, "he clearly keeps the roads in good nick."

"All the better for us."

The trees peter out into lush pasture. Carly insists on stopping to find the apple tree. "You don't know when there's going to be any more food," she reminds Soraya. "In the book they don't stop again between here and the city."

"We're in the book."

"You know what I mean."

They pick a couple of apples each for the journey and stash them in the bike basket, wrapped in Soraya's scarf to mitigate bruising. And they each eat one before they move off again, sitting on the velvety grass under the tree.

"One thing that worries me," Soraya says, "is what happens when we get there. And whether anyone's going to try to stop us getting there, if it comes to that."

Carly grins. "I don't think they will."

"Why not?"

"Because we have to get there. Because it just doesn't work if we don't. And because nobody cares how we do it, because nobody sees us."

This turns out to be a bit overoptimistic—they do, in fact, get seen by a washerwoman, a guard patrol, and a flock of geese, but they are faster than all of them.

"Though I could have done without the geese," Soraya pants.

The ground has been rising gently but steadily ever since they left the forest. Now the gradient gets steeper. It's becoming a proper hill. Carly stops the bike.

"Sorry," she says, "I can't go any further with both of us."

"Fair enough." Soraya slides off the back. "Shall I push it?"

"We're nearly there, anyway."

"Are we?"

"Yes. Remember: *as they reached the crest of the hill, another revealed itself to them, and on top of that peak was the glorious sight of the city.* Or something like that."

"Uphill all the way, then."

"Downhill on the way back."

"I guess so." They haven't speculated about what happens afterwards, not to each other. Carly's very afraid that the answer might be *nothing*. At best, it'll be a long slog back to the prison where they began, hoping that whatever it was that deposited them there will have the manners to pick them up again.

These gloomy thoughts take them up the hillside and, as promised, the city's there above them. And it is a truly lovely sight, its rooftops glittering in the sunlight, and red and blue pennants fluttering in the breeze.

"Well," Soraya says, "this is it."

"Yup. My turn to push?"

Carly isn't sure how long it takes them to climb the last stretch of road. It's as wide and as smooth as ever, but the gradient is still too steep to ride with a passenger. But at last they're there, in front of the great gate.

It's guarded heavily, but the door is open. Soraya hails the chief of the guard in an unsteady voice. "Greetings, friend. Have we leave to enter the city?"

"What's your business? And what's that device you have there?" He peers suspiciously at the bicycle, as if expecting it to explode. Carly wonders whether they should have left it at the bottom of the hill.

Then inspiration strikes. "We've come to earn our bread by entertaining the city folk. Why, when you see what we can do with this . . ."

He looks unconvinced. Thinking that it would be as well to make her point with actions rather than words, Carly mounts the bicycle and rides a couple of circles in front of the gate.

"Witchcraft. . . ." the man mutters as she dismounts.

No. Probably best not to be witches. Carly shakes her head. "No witchcraft, sir. Just mechanics. May we go in?"

He looks them both up and down, presumably looking for weapons, then nods. "Go on, then. But I hope you'll remember us poor guards on your way out."

"You'll have half of everything we make today," Carly promises extravagantly.

He looks less convinced than ever, but he orders the men to fall back.

"Good thinking," Soraya murmurs, as they pass under the arch.

It's easy enough to find the market square. There's a bustle of traders and customers, and enough space between the stalls to serve as a stage. The bike is already drawing curious glances, and when Carly gets on it once again, they've already got an admiring audience, even though all she's doing is riding in circles.

Soraya stands there for a moment, then starts shouting. "Roll up! Roll up! See . . . Carly the Fearless . . . and her magnificent . . . metal horse!"

There's a patter of applause. Carly smiles and waves. Soraya gestures at her to slow down and, when she comes to a stop, removes three apples from the basket with a comical air of surprise—and starts juggling with them. Carly's own look of surprise isn't faked. She starts riding again, tracing a circle around Soraya. More applause. Encouraged, she pulls a wheelie. The crowd's getting bigger and bigger, but she knows they can't keep doing this all afternoon. She slows to a stop in front of Soraya, puts both feet down, and bows deeply. Soraya hops onto the rack and cries, "Go! Go!"

"Now what?" Carly mutters as she pushes off again.

"Keep the act going just a little longer," Soraya replies. She's doing something. Carly can't see what. Something with the apples, perhaps. Yes: suddenly a child at the front of the crowd is holding one and looking rather dubious about it. Something red flashes past Carly's face, and Soraya lurches, swears, and falls off. The abrupt shift in the weight throws Carly, too, and suddenly she's on the ground with the bike on top of her. The crowd's laughing. And Soraya's speaking.

"Ladies and gentlemen . . . thank you! Thank you very much! It's a pleasure to be here. But we don't just have entertainment for you. We have news! Isn't that right?"

Carly picks herself up. "That's right! Someone far more exciting than us is on the way, and you'd better get ready to welcome him!

The man you know as—" oh, come on, what was the wording from the book?—"the Mountain Lord, the Hidden King, the One Who Wields the Emerald Scepter!"

The crowd stops laughing. There's some sharp, subdued conversation. It occurs to her that maybe this wasn't the greatest idea, what with the city being under the control of the usurping ruler and all.

Soraya's telling them: "Your true heir is on the way to this city. He'll be here at sunset. And so I ask you: How will you welcome him? Will you drive him away with sticks and stones? Or will you have the gates open and the banners flying? Will you escort him to the palace, so that he can take his place on his rightful throne? The choice is—"

And everything goes dark.

She's back at the bike rack. Alone. She's clutching the book in her hand. She doesn't dare open it again.

The bike's there, locked up securely. There's something red in the basket. She makes herself look, but she always knew it was going to be an apple.

Now what?

"Carly!" Soraya's voice carries across the square.

She turns round, knowing she's grinning. "Nice to see you!"

Soraya hurries over and, unexpectedly, hugs her. "Oh, thank goodness. I thought you'd got stuck there, and it would all have been my fault, picking that stupid book. . . . Then I remembered that you didn't arrive until I'd been there a couple of hours, and so maybe you wouldn't get back until later, too. . . ."

Carly stops her. "We fixed it. That was a good speech."

"Thanks. That was a brilliant idea, being street entertainers." Soraya still looks a bit dazed. She nods slowly. "I could do with a coffee."

"That does sound good," Carly says wistfully.

"Come on. My treat. Maybe a piece of Bakewell tart, too."

They get coffee and Bakewell tart and a table near the door where they can watch the students and tourists drifting past, reassuringly normal. Soraya stirs sugar into her cup. Carly lays the book on the table. She's just wondering how to pick up *this* conversation when someone behind her exclaims in astonishment.

"Good grief," the woman says.

They look round.

She might be in her fifties; she has grey hair in a bun, and she's wearing an olive-green quilted jacket. "I don't think I've ever met anyone else who's read that one. Did you, er, get all the way to the end?"

They glance at each other, smiling, eyebrows raised. "We did," Soraya says.

"I'd be very interested to hear *how*." Her tone is cautious.

Hesitantly, Soraya reaches into her pocket and pulls out one perfect red apple.

The woman nods. "Oh, yes. I remember those."

Carly laughs. "Come and sit with us," she says, "and we'll tell you everything."

THE PRICE THE HEART DEMANDS

✑ Jamie Perrault ✑

"**A**s you can see, officers . . ." Val spreads their hands, just resisting the urge to turn in a circle. They've very carefully curated their appearance for today—black trousers to go with a brightly colored wrap-around top that is loose and flowing enough to make it impossible to tell if Val has curves or not. They're using female pronouns on their ship's captain documentation right now, but that doesn't mean they have to like being aggressively gendered. "We're here for a bit of bicycling." *Nothing to get your good selves upset about*, the part of Val that grew up on holodramas wants to add, but they keep those words locked behind their teeth.

One of the pair of Natural Citizen spaceport authorities frowns at Val. "I'll be the one to determine that." Tanzen, his name tag reads, and Val steps aside to allow him better access to their cargo bay and the crates there.

Tanzen's partner yawns, which is less ideal than her being charmed by Val but still better than the absolute fervor with which Tanzen is pursuing his job.

Val gestures grandly at their equipment again, then forces themself to stand back and not fidget. Even though bored people fidget, too, they need to appear as calm and innocent as possible.

Tanzen rifles through the packs that go with the bikes, a frown etching itself deeper into his face with each one opened. "Why are there so many books?"

"What, don't you like reading?" Val's voice doesn't change at all, though their heart beats a little bit faster in their chest.

With a bright *meow*, Dream-Ring jumps up onto Val's shoulder, bright blue fur drawing the eye. It gives an excuse for Val's change in heart rate, something that should mask their slipup should either Tanzen or his partner be bothering to measure biometrics.

"There's liking reading, and then there's carrying . . . what, six books each?" The man bares his teeth in an expression that clearly isn't meant to be a smile. "You could fit twenty times that onto an e-reader. Save your backs some trouble, no?"

"E-readers don't support Indril, which is what these are written in." Val allows their voice to go just a little chilly as they reach up to pet Dream-Ring's ears. The six-legged cat purrs loudly as she butts against Val's hand. "Open one of the books and see. The diacritical marks are necessary to understand what's being said."

The man does open one of the books, flipping through it and grimacing in distaste.

"Come on, Zen." Tanzen's partner laconically picks up a second book, confirming Val's story with her own eyes. "There's nothing wrong with their documents. Let the tourists ride their bikes and read their books."

"Thank you." Val places their hand on their heart and gives a little bow. "Can I tell my companions that we're free to go, then?"

Tanzen hems and haws a bit more, but within ten minutes, Val has the necessary paperwork completed and electronically filed. They're able to move from the cargo hold back up to the bridge with the news the rest of the crew has been desperately waiting for.

"We're good." Val gives a little *oof* as Dream-Ring jumps from their shoulder to Kura's.

Kura closes her eyes, burying her fingers in Dream-Ring's fur and sighing silently. "Shall we get started, then?"

Nobody argues. The crew has been cooped up for the last three weeks. The ship is a very nice one by any standards, but getting a chance to use their legs—or in Byron's case, his arms— will be an appreciated change of pace.

The spaceport is bustling, people coming and going, unloading cargo and arguing in a variety of languages.

The most commonly spoken one is Endri, though. Which shouldn't be as troubling to Val as it is—Endri is the founding planetary language here, and anywhere the Natural Citizens have taken power isn't going to be kind to multiculturalism. They'll tolerate tourists speaking their own languages, but only so long as it's among themselves, and only so long as it's not an inconvenience to anyone else. For trade, for the creation of actual relationships—

"Smile, Val." Kura's admonition comes along with a smile.

Would anyone else here know that it's fake? Know that it's a more bitter version of the smile that Kura brings to every bedside of every person she's going to have to give bad news to? Surely the rest of the crew does. Byron probably remembers this smile from Kura's telling him he'd never walk without assistance again. But all these people on the port authority, all these people they're trying to wend their way through . . .

"Come on, loves." Val's smile is all teeth, their voice projecting bright determination. Does their crew understand what that means? Does *Val* know what it means, that the easy charisma they bring to all their missions is failing? "Let's see what this world has to offer."

Val pushes their bike through the combination of new steel and well-worn metal that is the spaceport, hearing the familiar *ting-ting-ting* of bicycle spokes. The crew could have brought something less vintage—something that would require less physical work—but it wouldn't have functioned as well with their cover story.

Also, it wouldn't be nearly as fun.

Once they're free of the spaceport, everyone mounts up, falling into their usual formation. Drawing in a deep breath of Oslin's air—a breath that tastes different from any other planet Val has been on, because *every* planet has its own unique bite—Val looks to Dream-Ring. "Which way, fluff-tail?"

Dream-Ring arches, bright blue eyes fixing Val for a moment before the cat turns imperiously to point east.

East they shall go, then.

Val starts pedaling, and everything else dissolves into wind and sun and the need to be *moving*, always moving, onward to a destination that they could, sadly, find just about anywhere in the galaxy.

∽ • ∽

Dream-Ring leads them to a town two days' journey from the spaceport.

The Natural Citizens clearly hold power here, their sun-and-shield sigil branded on everything from the post office to the bakery. No genetically engineered flours used here, even though they cut the rate of childhood vitamin deficiencies by at least 60 percent.

Val at first tries not to step into any buildings where the sign is visible, but it soon becomes clear that it won't be possible to avoid them all. Not when the crew needs food, a selection of local clothing to use when necessary, and to pop into enough tourist destinations to look like reasonable travelers rather than illicit doctors.

The crew has settled into their first hostel within half a day, exchanging tidbits that they've discovered about the city. Val knows they should stay in the main room with the crew, should listen, should help plan matters out, but they still find themself following Dream-Ring out onto the balcony and staring in the same direction the cat stares.

"The hospital's over there." Kura's voice startles Val, and they look over just in time to see Kura nodding towards where a large building, at least twenty stories tall, dominates the horizon. "That's probably what attracted Dream-Ring."

The cat yawns, displaying razor-sharp teeth.

Val turns fully, looking through the open balcony door to study their crew. The six of them seem so alert, so focused. Do they all realize that they're touching their packs—touching the precious books contained in the waterproof packaging, and the medicine that hides inside? "Are we ready to move out?"

Kura nods. "Nothing more we can do until we find some people to help us. Some people who need us enough that they're willing to . . ."

To risk everything, most likely because the alternative is death. Though there's always the chance they'll find people like themselves—people who are willing to do the right thing *because* it's the right thing. "We want to search together or separate?"

If they'd been able to get a good contact system set up here . . . but if they'd been able to get a legal contact system together, Val's crew wouldn't be here. Even an *illegal* contact system would have likely attracted a different crew.

Val's people are the ones who go in when no one else can. When no one else *will*.

"Separate." Byron's the one who answers. "Less likelihood of the whole team being picked up."

"Pairs." Kura's eyes narrow.

"Pairs it is." Val knows when to push their second-in-command and when not to. "Who wants Dream-Ring?"

The cat lunges off of Val's shoulder, wrapping all six legs around Val's head and clinging tight.

Byron is the first to laugh, but definitely not the only one. "Don't worry, little kitty. We all know where you belong."

Dream-Ring chirrups but doesn't actually move off of Val's head and back to their shoulder until the rest of the crew has left the building, riding off into the city on their bikes.

Val swings into their seat. Releasing the brake on their bike, Val points at Dream-Ring's chest. "Earn your keep today, little beast."

Dream-Ring promptly bites Val's finger before butting their head against Val's until Val turns west down one of the side streets that leads towards the hospital quarter.

Val doesn't hesitate to follow the cat's suggestion, leading Kura deep into the shadow of the city and all of the broken dreams it hides out of sight.

ᗢ • ᗣ

"This is illegal." The woman—mother—looks down at the page that Val has carefully pulled from one of their books.

"Only here." Kura's words are low, gentle, and cajoling.

Val keeps their lips shut tight around any clarifying statements. These people—these frightened parents—undoubtedly know that *only here* means anywhere the Natural Citizens have power. Anywhere it's illegal to alter your body, illegal to use anything that touches God's precious building blocks—anywhere it's illegal to hold beliefs in a kinder, more understanding, more *caring* God than the vicious autocrat that helps the Natural Citizens keep power. At the moment, that's about 52 percent of all populated worlds.

"It will . . ." The father looks back towards where the child they're discussing—a little thing, only four years old—is sleeping. "It'll fix her?"

Kura nods. "A drop of blood here, to allow for activation and specialization. Give the apparatus an hour to fully actualize, dissolve it in sterile water, and inject it under the skin. Your daughter's leukemia will be cured."

"By permanently altering her DNA." The mother places a hand over her mouth, muffling her own voice. "Will they be able to tell?"

"There are certain tests that could give the procedure away, especially if carried out within the next six Terran months." Kura looks between the parents. "But it's safe and effective. It's been used for over a decade on worlds the Natural Citizens don't control. I've had it done to myself. Can you tell by looking at me?"

The two parents stare hard at Kura, taking in every inch of her exposed skin, looking at her eyes from a hundred different subtle angle shifts.

They *want* there to be something there. They want to be able to say that what was done stole some intrinsic part of Kura, because if it didn't—if she's fine—then their child has been suffering needlessly for months.

Some would chase Kura off at this point. For some people, holding tight to their illusions is more important than holding tight to their lives and their loves.

For most people, though: "Please help us do it, then." It's the father who reaches forward first, but the mother's hands are close behind. "Please, we'll give you whatever payment you want. Just don't let our little girl die."

Kura doesn't have to be asked twice. With quick, practiced movements, she pricks the child's finger, allowing a drop of blood to fall onto the activation strip—onto the title and author, printed at the top of each page of biofilm. Then she begins the careful step-by-step instructions of how to inject the solution—instructions that the father interrupts. "Can't you do it?"

The mother nods, too, holding her child and rocking the little one back and forth, back and forth.

For their part, the child seems more fascinated than frightened by what's going on. A bandage pulses light red on the tip of their finger, a simple repeating holo of a fire-breathing dragon sliding on one corner and off the other.

When the child sees Val watching, they bury their head against their mother's shoulder.

There's so much Val wants to tell the little one—so much they want to shout at the parents, who have clearly swallowed at least part of the Natural Citizen's propaganda.

Or perhaps they've all just been born in the wrong place, at the wrong time, and Val just wants to shout at the universe that all this is unfair.

Kura's hand catches Val's, and Val looks down into Kura's eyes.

They can't afford to stay here for the hour it will take to get everything done. That's an hour they could be trying to find others to help—an hour during which this family could decide to do something stupid and turn them in.

Val sighs, inclining their head the smallest bit.

Dream-Ring jumps down from their shoulder, leaping into the child's lap and butting against their head. With a delighted squeal of joy, the little one wraps their arms around Dream-Ring and squeezes.

Val smiles at Dream-Ring's look of long-suffering sorrow. What did the silly thing expect? Children will always be children.

Settling down on the floor in front of the child, Val decides that they're spending the next hour trying to teach the little one as much as they can before the parents shut Val up.

Maybe it will be enough to make the lost time worthwhile.

൚ • ൙

Val finds what they need by following a thread from the fourth desperate person they save.

Doctor Carov fidgets in his chair, his long surgeon's fingers wrapped around the glass that Kura provided. The room they're in is cheap, a tiny space in a soaring skyscraper designed to pack as many tourists as possible into the smallest footprint.

Dream-Ring leaps into the man's lap, purring and rubbing against Carov's chin. Fur drifts down to land in his drink.

Kura smiles, patting the man on the shoulder as she maneuvers to sit with Val on the bed. If Dream-Ring likes the man, he means them no harm.

Val leans forward. "You've been telling people to look into medical procedures that are illegal."

Carov takes a drink, closing his eyes. "I've been telling people the truth."

"We know." Kura's voice is all gentle reassurance. "We understand."

"We can help." Val resists the urge to reach out and grab the man. They've been doing this long enough; they know when things can't be rushed. That doesn't mean they don't want to rush them—that they're not tired of the song that has to go before the dance. "We have enough treatments prepared for nine thousand people, give or take. We can also leave information if you have people who could recreate the pages."

Carov swallows, still with his eyes closed. "What's your price?"

"No price." Kura's voice cools several degrees. "We're Riders. This is what we do."

"Riders?" Carov's shoulders drop noticeably, and he studies Kura and Val with a new eagerness. "You mean . . . Medical Riders?"

Val glances at Kura. "Is that what all those papers we signed meant? I thought we were just promising to wear our helmets and obey local safety laws."

Kura swats at Val's arm without moving her eyes from Carov. "We're a special branch, if you will. We go where we're not technically invited. Because people need medical care whether their governments will allow it or not."

"That's true. I've always been impressed with the Riders. A ship and a bike and a bag . . ." Carov tentatively smiles between the two of them. "Is it wonderful?"

Val considers, tilting their head. "It's what we need to do. There are moments of wonder, yes." There's a little one who's going to live now, and remember, and hopefully change something for their world.

"What do you want me to do?" Carov's hands begin shaking, his eyes flitting from Val to Kura.

"Do you know other people who would help? In cities we can reach?" Val pulls out a pen and paper—old tools, but sometimes they're safer.

Finally removing one hand from his glass, Carov rubs at the back of his neck. "I . . . I don't know. But I can try? Give you some names?"

"That's a good starting point." Kura's tone softens again, taking on a slightly pleading quality. "Anything you can tell us—every little bit helps."

Every little bit makes it less likely they'll be found—less likely they'll either be killed or deported. Just like Dream Ring's senses provide a bit of extra safety, this man's assistance will make it more likely they're able to help as many people as they came prepared to assist.

Drawing in a deep breath, Carov squares his shoulders and begins giving names.

Val writes them down, a quick, neat column in Indril that will hopefully spell the difference between success and failure.

༅ • ༄

The rides between cities are Val's favorite.

They don't always take their bikes. Some distances are just better covered via mass transportation. People aren't meant to live cut off from the worlds they call home, though. They're meant to breathe in the air—and this air is delightful. It's not always. Many of the worlds they visit have seen more than their fair share of trauma and tribulations. It's not uncommon for a chemical undertone to taint every breath.

Oslin hasn't been in Natural Citizen hands for long, though. The election that toppled anything approaching democracy happened less than thirty years ago. The roads between cities— roads designed for cyclists and pedestrians, not for individual transports—are still being maintained.

Dream-Ring rides on Val's shoulder, head high, claws dug deep into the jacket that Val always wears when cycling long distances.

Their ears are pricked, their body relaxed, no sign of worry or fear. Without Dream-Ring, these missions would be practically suicide. The little blue cat, so sensitive to other's emotions, has kept Val safe through more trials than Val cares to admit.

Kura huffs up beside Val, her skin slick with sweat. "I think we can cut the pace a bit, Captain. You're leaving everyone in the dust."

Val glances back over their shoulder, surprised to see their crew spread out in a long tail behind them. "Right, let's call it a break for lunch anyway."

They pull off to the side of the road, standing their bikes in the purple grass and passing out sandwiches and wraps. The meal passes in a rush of easy banter and quick jokes, everyone seeming pleased with the progress they've made so far.

They should be. If the contacts from Carov are to be believed, they'll be greeted by a group of 369 patients in the next city, all of them well prepared for what Val and company can offer.

If Carov's doctor friends made mistakes. . . .

Kura's hand lands on Val's shoulder, and they lean into the touch without thinking.

"You're too nervous. You're never this nervous." Kura's words are soft, for Val's ears only. "What's wrong?"

"We've been doing this for years." Val doesn't allow the slight smile on their face to fade. "And things aren't improving."

"They are for the people we help." Kura's fingers tighten, a fierce grip.

"I know. Which is why nothing's wrong." Val pops the rest of their wrap into their mouth, savoring the rice with its unfamiliar spices. "Or at least, nothing more than usual."

Kura frowns, but she moves away, back to her own bike and her own burdens.

Val gives their crew a few more minutes to relax, and then kicks their bike into gear once more.

Nothing is wrong except what has always been wrong—that people are foolish, and selfish, and willing to let their neighbor suffer so long as they don't have to see it. That people will fear what they don't understand. That people will accept oppression so long as they feel someone else—some ill-defined enemy—is bearing the brunt of that oppression.

Just like nothing is right except what has always been right—that some people will help, and most people want the world to be fair, and the vast majority of people have kindness at their core.

It's been enough to keep Val and Dream-Ring and Kura and the others moving so far, and it's going to have to keep being enough, because the worlds haven't stopped needing them yet.

⌒ • ⌒

Things go about as well as they could hope.

They see patient after patient. They talk scared, nervous people through a procedure that most of them would have sworn they'd never consider prior to actually needing it.

They see cancer patients, lupus patients, patients with a myriad of illnesses, all of whom can be helped by the pages in their books. They tear out page after page, marking them with blood, activating the science inside.

They save lives, and all it takes is the risk of their own.

Dream-Ring stays close to Val, refusing to leave even when they would better serve someone else on the crew. It's proof that Val's being too maudlin, that their own emotional regulation isn't working, and it irritates Val even as they appreciate the press of paws against their shoulders, the warm purring against their stomach at night.

They make a circle through the most populous continent on Oslin, visiting fourteen cities and the countryside between. They finish back where they started, in New Endri, with Carov and the people he has summoned to receive their forbidden treatment.

It's a very different experience this time. Carov may be a nervous man, but he has a good heart and plenty of funds, and that can be made to move mountains. Instead of meeting in small hostel rooms, Val's crew has the whole of a hotel dance floor to themselves. Music pours from the walls and the ceiling, surrounding everyone in a comforting bubble of sound. Chairs are arranged in the open space, and family groups huddle together, almost always surrounding the person needing treatment.

The next boy on Val's list isn't the only one alone. There are quite a few others in his age range—late teens, early twenties—who don't have a protective group around them. They're the ones who are here despite their family and friends not wanting them to be—the ones who are unwilling to be martyrs for others' causes.

Val approaches him, their last near-empty book held tight against their chest by their right arm. They gesture for the boy to follow them, and lead him towards two chairs that are set close together.

"What do you need?" Val tries to ask the question gently, but when you've asked anything a thousand times it tends to come out rough.

The boy glances around uneasily before leaning forward. "To be like you."

Val frowns, too confused to be wary. "I'm sorry? You want to be a Rider?"

Shaking his head, the boy points at Val's chest and then at their chin. "To be like *you*. You're not a proper sex, are you?"

Val bristles, instantly on guard. "Who told you to come here?"

"No one." The boy blanches, hands rising defensively. "I'm not—I don't want to cause trouble. I want what you have. Please. I want my body to be *right*."

The fight flows out of Val as quickly as it arrived. "Oh, child."

Now it's the boy's turn to bristle. "I'm not a *child*. I'm nineteen. I'm an adult, and I know what I want."

"If I give you something like what I took—" Val presses their hand against their chest, flattening their clothes to show there are no breasts despite there being no hair growing on their chin. "Then you lose everything you have here. They don't allow anything other than binary sex on this planet. Intersex children are—"

"Eliminated in utero or fixed when they're born. I know." The boy's chin rises, and Val sees something familiar in his eyes. "That's what they did to me. My mother didn't get properly tested, and when I was born *wrong* they corrected me to what they thought I should be. But they didn't get it right, and I . . . I can't spend my whole life like this."

Val recognizes the desperation in the boy's voice. They've seen it on a dozen different worlds; they've heard it from a hundred different historical holos. They never had to feel it themself—they were always allowed to be what and who they are.

They can't offer this child what they need. They can't undo whatever butchery was done. The pages that they have aren't keyed for sex reassignment. The pages won't recognize the problem and will have just as much of a chance of making things worse as making them better.

"Why haven't you tried to leave?" The words come out as a weak whisper.

"And go where? With who?" The young one's words crack up an octave. "It takes money for transport. Money for paperwork. Money for *everything*, and I don't have enough. Please, please—I'll do whatever you need, whatever you ask, just . . . please. Give me a body like yours."

Val stands, and the young one draws back, almost knocking their chair over backward.

Dream-Ring leaps from Val's shoulder without being asked. They move over to the young one, reaching out to sniff them before giving an imperious *mraow*.

"Do you really mean you'll give up anything? Your whole world? Everyone you know?" Val keeps their voice ice-cold.

The child swallows, closing their eyes, and the pain in their shoulders should belong to someone much older. "I'd rather be able to stay here, but it'll kill me. I can *feel* it killing me. So yes. If that's the cost . . . yes."

It shouldn't be. No one should have to choose between their home and their survival.

Val knows how little "shouldn't be" controls the universe, though. "Then pack your bags. I'm going to give you an address to meet us at, and we're going to get you offworld, somewhere that you can properly be fixed."

The young one's eyes light up. "Thank you! Thank you!"

"Don't thank me. Just show up, and think of what name you want to use, because you're going to have to leave the old one behind." Val takes a piece of normal paper and writes down the rendezvous point, turning away from the young one to finish their job.

The rest of the crew will understand.

"We don't smuggle people!" Kura paces from one end of their campsite to the other. "That's one of the few rules we have! We don't smuggle people—it puts too big a target on our backs."

Dream-Ring curls around Val's neck, purring loudly. "We're smuggling this person."

"Why?" Byron rocks his bike back and forth, back and forth. "What about this kid's worth risking a mission that's gone great so far? If we don't do this, we can come back in three months and make another round. We can keep helping people."

"If we don't get caught, we can keep doing that. People disappear all the time." Val doesn't move, needing to be a stable point to counter Kura's nerves. "They'll have no reason to blame us if we can get the kid on the ship without anyone noticing."

Kura puts her head in her hands and screams, a muffled sound that still cuts through Val.

"Why do you need to do this?" Byron rolls a little bit closer, staring into Val's eyes. "Why this kid? Why now?"

"Because if I don't help them, I'm not going to be coming back on any future missions." The truth tumbles out before Val is even certain they're going to be able to say it. "Because we're doing good, but we're also fighting a battle we shouldn't have to fight, and it's meaning I leave people like me—people like this desperate, hurt kid—to continue to suffer. That we prioritize everyone else's hurt and pain because there's *more* of them, because people like this kid can just continue to live in misery, because . . . because . . ."

"Because we can't win all the battles that need to be fought. That *should* be fought." Kura stops her pacing in front of Val. Reaching out, she twines their fingers together. "Because we're fighting the one we can win right now, and not the one that you need."

"I like the battle we're fighting right now." Val waits for Dream-Ring to shift so that they can lean forward and press against Kura. "It's important. It matters. But this matters to me too. I know it's just one person. I know it's not some great blow. But it's going to be enough for me."

"Or at least not doing it will be too much." Kura's arms are strong as they hug Val tight. "All right, then. Who here's got an idea how we're smuggling the captain's new pet aboard?"

And just like that, the decision is made. No one else protests again. They just start brainstorming what they can do with the resources they have, and where they can take the kid once they've got them safely off planet.

The Medical Rider board likely won't be as easy to sway as Val's crew, but that's a battle for another day. Right now, they've already bitten off more than they might be able to swallow.

◦ • ◦

"Friends." Val spreads their hands, palms up. "Are we really going to do this again?"

It's not the same two guards, of course. That would be too much serendipity. But the faces and disposition of the people responsible for allowing them egress from the planet look so much like the ones who wanted to deny them access that Val can't help themself.

"Open the boxes, please." The frownier man steps forward, his hand on a baton.

With a flourishing bow Val does just that, keying the first crate to open for inspection. This one is stacked high with books, all of them actual paper, the gamut of languages they cover impressive given the short time Byron had to find them.

The guard spends twenty minutes, steadily more and more annoyed, going through each and every book, flipping through the pages, finding absolutely nothing of interest.

The second crate is filled with bicycle parts. The guards look at each other before diving in.

The third crate opens to reveal another set of parts.

The fourth opens with a soft click to reveal yet more books.

"Open the last one." The second guard looks harried as he presses forward, getting a view of more bicycle parts in the fifth crate, these ones for a custom build for Byron.

"All right." The first guard makes only a cursory stab into the second box of books, pulling up a tome with a blue leather cover and letting it fall. "Enjoy your books and your bikes."

"We will." Val smiles and gives a little wave as they guide their cargo through the scanners and towards the waiting ship.

The scanners aren't a problem. By scraping together all of their funds, the crew had bought a reflective cover for Tuoma that would make them look like yet more books. The danger had been the guards.

They still wait until the ship is off planet and beyond the reach of any orbital weapons to unpack the young adult.

Tuoma sits up hesitantly, stretching out the kinks their confinement caused. "Are we through?"

"We're through." Val props themself on another crate, watching their new charge. "You're free. As soon as it's safe I'll contact our friends at Medical Riders, and they'll get you set up for whatever type of body mod you need to feel comfortable. Beyond that, I'm afraid I can't offer you much."

"You're already offering me more than anyone else has." Tuoma's eyes fill with tears, and they brush them away hurriedly. "Thank you. I'll make it up to you somehow. I promise."

"You don't owe me anything." Val reaches up to scratch Dream-Ring's ears. "All you have to do is live, all right? That's all any of us have to do—keep living."

Tuoma studies them, head tilting slightly. "I would have thought you'd want me to promise to help other people like us. To, you know, pass it forward."

"If you feel up to that, I'd love to see you do it. If you've got the temperament and the drive to be a Rider, to go out and do what needs to be done, then please, go, do it. Heavens know there aren't enough people who step up." Val gives a little *oof* as Dream-Ring bounces from their shoulder over to Tuoma. "But that's not something you owe anyone. That's something you do because you can. Because you *have* to. Because your heart won't let you not."

Tuoma nods slowly, scratching Dream-Ring under the chin. "Is that why you do it? Because your heart won't let you stop?"

The answer to that is so very complicated. Val could stop. There are days when it feels like they *should* stop, like they're getting too old or too tired or too sad to keep going.

But if they stop, who will step forward to risk what Val risks? Who will protect their crew?

Who will decide, when confronted with someone like Tuoma, that they can't live with themself if they do nothing?

"I do it because I can." It's a true enough answer. "And I'll do it for as long as I can."

"Then maybe one day we'll ride together." Tuoma smiles hesitantly. "Though I'm no good on a bike right now."

"You've got time to learn." Val levers themself up, and Dream-Ring comes scampering back to their regular perch. "That's what I've bought you. Do what you need to do with it."

Val knows that Tuoma is trailing behind them as they head back to the bridge, but they don't turn to look.

There are stars to navigate, bicycles to build, books to fill with new potentials and new stories.

Kura hands over the controls. "Where to, Captain?"

"Where we're always headed." Val caresses the ship that will bring them to another world. "To a better future, by whatever ways we need to take to get there."

Kura doesn't answer in words, but her hands snake around to hug Val from behind, and that's all the confirmation Val needs right now to know they're on the right path.

THE WILD RIDE
∾ *Shelby Schwieterman* ∾

Carly wasn't upset, and she didn't care what the other girls thought of her. She simply wanted to read her book more than she wanted to participate in some stupid sleepover, and if that made enemies for her, then so be it. What could a group of sixth grade girls do to her anyway? Gossip about her at school? Ha, like that could harm her. Carly was tough. Carly was a freaking Crystal Warrior, just like Annabeth the Quick, hero of the Shining Realm, protector of the Great Egg of Wisdom.

Carly paused under a street lamp to adjust the straps of her backpack. She had perfected the art of reading while walking back in, like, fourth grade, but doing it at night really upped the difficulty level. Her right hand ached from holding the book open and turning pages with her thumb; her left hand was slippery with sweat where it gripped the cell phone she used as a reading light. She longed for the return of her actual reading light, which had been taken away after she'd been caught too many times reading under her covers while she should have been sleeping.

The night was hot and humid for this time of year. Crickets chirped happily while toads croaked and sang, trying to outdo the little insects. Carly had been a sixth grader for almost two months now—the very least the weather could do would be to reward her with a cool, breezy night in which to walk home. It was the time of year for ghost stories and black cats and strange whispers on the wind, not for sweating through your pajamas and daydreaming about snow.

"Ugh," Carly said to the undesirable weather. She balanced the phone on the book, wiped her sweaty palm, shook out her other hand, and then continued on.

Most people walking home from an abandoned sleepover at sometime after midnight would stick to the sidewalk. Not Carly. The empty street provided a wider, clearer path for her feet to follow while her eyes were busy finishing chapter twelve so she could get to chapter thirteen in which Annabeth breaks the other Crystal Warriors out of the dungeon so they can help her find the Great Egg, which has been stolen by the evil emperor's dark forces.

Some people would be worried about being hit by cars, but this scene was one of Carly's favorites, and she hadn't seen or heard any cars since she started her walk home ten minutes ago. Some people, in Carly's opinion, were just too cautious. How could anyone enjoy the book they were reading if they were constantly worrying about what was going on around them while they read?

Except for the occasional runaway or missing person, Carly's town was quiet and boring. Just like Carly, according to the girls at the sleepover. Carly didn't take it to heart. Those girls simply could not stand that they were less interesting than a book she had read a dozen times already. Her copy of *The Crystal Warriors* was beginning to look like it had been through as many battles as the Crystal Warriors themselves. The paperback cover was chipped and bent from being shoved into and ripped out of a backpack, a bookshelf, a desk, and a hiding place behind a different book so her teachers wouldn't know she was reading it again instead of "expanding her horizons." The pages were soft and feathery from dirt and oils they'd collected with each turn. Pages 13, 86, and 184 were marked with fingerprints of cheese dust from Carly's careless snacking while reading. An unfortunate blotch of spaghetti sauce graced page 92, not to be confused with the actual bloodstain on page 93, the result of a sudden but minor nosebleed. It was as if she had left almost as much of herself in the book as the book had left in her. Almost.

As Carly's feet slapped the pavement, she turned the page. Chapter thirteen. *Yes!* Carly's pace quickened as she followed Annabeth sneaking into Fort Marion's hidden underground prison, subduing guards before they even realize they're not alone. She was called Annabeth the Quick not because of her fast feet, but because of her fast thinking. She could talk her way out of trouble and talk others *into* trouble with fluid reasoning and endless charm. Of any character in the book, Annabeth had the best insults *and* the best comebacks. She was about to deliver one of her wittiest to a prison guard when—

The phone light flickered, then died, plunging Carly and her book into the thick dark of the night. Carly wiped sweat off her forehead with the back of her arm. After a few misses, she managed to tuck her phone into a pocket of her backpack. Something about the night felt wrong. Carly turned slowly in the street, searching for whatever felt so off about the darkness. She squinted, but couldn't see the streetlight she'd passed just moments before. The only light came from the moon and stars above. Definitely too little to read by.

"Ugh," she said to the darkness. She'd have to walk the rest of the way without reading. Doable, but not preferable. Even the toads and crickets were mad about it. She could tell because they were unusually silent, except for a strange whirring whine from somewhere back the way she came.

As Carly stood there, perplexed, the darkness at the end of the street transitioned to a milky green glow that moved quickly toward her. The long, whining sound grew louder. Sudden wind whipped her hair around her face, obscuring her vision, making her doubt that what she was seeing was real: Within the pale green light were cyclists. Dozens of them, maybe a hundred. They moved as a unit as they sped closer. Heads down, feet pumping, wheels spinning, frames rattling, they headed right for her. Carly couldn't tell where the riders ended and their bikes began. One figure led the pack, with the rest following in a swarm. She blinked, and they were yards away. She blinked again and they were upon her.

Cyclists zipped past, grazing her elbows and knocking her left and right. She caught a flash of yellow eyes, a glint of white teeth, an otherworldly grin. The din of at least a 100 wheels flying past was accented with manic, frenzied laughter and the smell of hot rubber.

Carly dropped to the ground in a crouch, her arms curling over her head for protection. She expected to be run over. She was faced with the entirely new reality that she might die at any time. And that time might be after midnight, in the dark, as strange glowing cyclists ran her over in the middle of the road.

This is not, she thought, *how a Crystal Warrior would get killed!* Her scream vibrated in her throat, more like a growl of frustration than an expression of terror. But before her growl ended, space opened up around her. The sound of bikes whizzed away down the road. She jumped to her feet and watched the herd of cyclists move farther and farther down the street, taking their glowing light with them.

For a moment, Carly was frozen with awe. Just for a moment. Soon, though, she realized something very important was missing. It wasn't in her hands, and it wasn't on the ground. Not even a scrap of paper or a chunk of cover remained. She checked her backpack, just to be sure. But no, it was gone.

Carly turned back toward the direction in which the herd had disappeared and shouted, "Give me back my book, you bicycle freaks!"

A dog barked at her in reply. Light had returned to the street, and Carly suspected that if she stood there too long, mourning the loss of her book, some insomniac neighbor would peek out their window and wonder why a little girl was standing in the middle of the street in the dark sometime after midnight.

She walked home in a daze, mourning and seething. Why would they take her book? Why couldn't they have taken literally anything else? If it had been anything else, she could have told her parents and classmates all about the strange experience. It could have become just another local legend.

Since it was her book, though, she'd have to find a way to get it back.

$\infty \cdot \infty$

Carly dreamt that night. She rode a bike in a crowd of faceless laughter. Wind caressed her cheeks and arms and pedaling feet as she and the rest of the herd flew up and over the town. They rode through the sky over a forest, over a river, over other towns full of people dreaming, just like they did every night. They touched down to the surface only now and then, in specific parts of specific towns—it was the time of year when they were more visible, and they liked to hide from most people. Most people weren't willing to part with the things the herd wanted.

As she rode, the breeze drying sweat at her temples, her fingers began to disappear, one by one. She kept riding. Her arms went next, then her legs.

Then, she was all gone.

〰 • 〰

Carly woke with a mission. She'd be going back to school the next day, and if she didn't have her book, she was going to die. She knew she wouldn't literally die, but she felt like she would. Sometimes feelings were more important than thoughts, like when Annabeth's brother Wynn could sense something was wrong with the Egg even though everyone else assumed it was safe and sound, exactly where it should be, not already stolen and replaced with a replica.

While Carly worked out her plan, both of her parents complained of strange dreams keeping them from sleeping restfully. Carly wondered if their dreams involved moonlight and bicycles and the slow disappearance of body parts. Her bike-riding nemeses must have had something to do with it. Did they want her to try to reach them? Did they pave this way for her?

Carly wasn't sure if the cyclists were fairies, ghosts, or something else, so she prepared a variety of supplies. In *The Crystal Warriors*, they dealt with a family of fairies who didn't like iron, so Carly swiped one of her dad's golf clubs from the garage. She hoped it was actually made of iron and not just called a nine iron for some other stupid reason. According to a television show she'd seen, ghosts would be taken care of with a container of salt from the kitchen. She also grabbed a bulb of garlic just in case. It was the 21st century—maybe vampires rode bicycles.

Her parents were a little suspicious after waking up that morning and finding Carly in her bed when she was supposed to be having fun at a slumber party like other little girls, but they weren't suspicious enough to fix the screen on her window, which easily and noiselessly popped out of its frame with very little effort on Carly's part. Channeling Annabeth's stealthy maneuvers from chapter thirteen, Carly slid out her window and into the grass at the side of the house just before 11:00 p.m.

Resting against the wall where she'd stashed it earlier in the day was an old bicycle. The frame was pink, the basket was crooked, and the handlebar tassels were reduced to a couple tangled strands of purple ribbon. She hadn't ridden it in at least two years, and it was too small and definitely too girly for her. Carly let herself feel embarrassed that a magical group of bicycle-riding creatures would see her with this pink hunk of junk, but only for a moment. She had work to do. She hopped on the bike, situated her supplies, and rode off toward the neighbor's house by the streetlight where she'd nearly died last night.

The night was cooler than the night before, but only barely. As Carly rode, the rushing air hit the sweat beading at her temples, evaporating and cooling. It was a nice sensation, like reading in bed or turning a page. How long would it take to master the art of reading while riding a bike? Was it even possible?

Before Carly could work out the logistics, she arrived at her destination. She was counting on the cyclists taking the same route they did the night before. They had to, otherwise how would she get her book back? She found that in situations of uncertainty, it was best to exert her will and demand things happen the way she wanted them to. Just like the Crystal Warriors when they jumped into the Cosmic Cloud of Wonder to retrieve the Great Egg. No one had ever gone into the cloud before, but it just had to work because it was the only way.

Carly hopped off the bike and let it fall onto the grass at the side of the road. She pulled the golf club out from where she'd tucked it between her back and her backpack and spent a moment brandishing it like a sword. She was a Crystal Warrior, and she was going to get her book back.

She grabbed the cylindrical tub of salt out of her backpack. It smelled like garlic. The whole backpack smelled like garlic. Carly wrinkled her nose. *No wonder vampires don't like it*. The salt tub had a convenient metal spout at the top. Carly pried it open, then poured a thick line right across the pavement. She made sure the line was visible and uninterrupted. No way were they getting past this masterpiece of ghost-proofing. She ripped apart the garlic bulb into its separate cloves, then placed them equidistant across the road, just next to the salt line.

Her preparation was complete. All that was left to do was wait. Carly sat cross-legged next to her bicycle, laid the golf club across her lap, and pulled a book from her backpack. She'd brought extras because of course she had. They were all nice books, but none had anywhere near the power of *The Crystal Warriors*. It was difficult for Carly to read anything else. Whenever she tried, she just thought, "Wow, I wish I were reading *The Crystal Warriors*."

She spent a few minutes attempting to read a lesser work of fiction by the light of her phone before giving up. She still had half an hour until midnight. What was she going to do for half an hour? A half hour was *forever*.

She scooted over to her bike and ran a finger along the greasy chain. She pushed on the pedal, and saw how its movement caused the wheels to move. She liked the simplicity of one movement leading to another. It was just like in *The Crystal Warriors*, when every step the warriors took was connected to the point before, but somehow it created this beautiful story. Point A: the Great Egg is stolen, or the pedal is pushed. Point B: the Crystal Warriors have a great adventure, or you're flying over asphalt with the wind evaporating the sweat at your temples.

When the whirring started, Carly didn't notice it. It was so faint at first, and the build was so gradual, that Carly didn't recognize it until the streetlight went out. Now she was in business. She hopped up and grabbed the golf club. Squinting down the road, she waited until she could see that green ghostly glow before extending the golf club out into the street. If her line of salt and garlic didn't work, she'd at least whack someone with iron.

The glow grew brighter, then resolved into the shapes of many cyclists. Carly got a better look now that she knew what she was looking at. She wished she hadn't. Maybe it was a trick of the light, or lack of it, but the riders' limbs all seemed a bit too long, like she was looking at them through the mirrors at the spring carnival from the place everyone called a "funhouse" but was not actually fun at all. Elbows and knees jostled other riders as each one fought for space on the narrow street. One figure in front seemed a bit larger than the rest. They were speeding closer to her, and they seemed to get faster as they approached. They were at the street corner, then the streetlight, then just feet away from her. That's when the larger one looked up and looked straight at her.

Carly screamed, then felt the impact against the golf club. It was wrenched from her grip as she fell backward into the grass, scraping her elbows on the edge of the sidewalk. As the group screamed by, her vision was flooded with the sight of that face that had looked up at her. Eyes and smiling teeth, a mane of black hair. The proportions all wrong, just so wrong. It was still looking at her, Carly felt. It looked at her with amusement, with curiosity. Carly wasn't sure she wanted that thing's attention.

But she did want her book, and she still didn't have it.

She sat up next to her bike. The golf club was nowhere in sight, gone just like her book. She didn't have long to think about it before the cyclists disappeared, but she was certain that she had only one option left. She would have to go in. She'd have to join that mass of writhing limbs and spinning wheels. She'd have to speak to them from inside their pack. It was the only way to know where her book had gone. And her dad's golf club, but she didn't really care about that.

It was dangerous. It was actually crazy. She knew that. But she couldn't stop obsessing over the idea. She had to go in. She was a warrior. She would make it out. She would rescue the book. She had to. She jumped on her bike.

Each pump of the pedals brought her closer to the climax of her story. She could tell this was it. Everything was moving uphill toward something, just like in a book. She was her book. The book was her. That's why she needed it back. She didn't want to lose a piece of herself.

She pumped those pedals as hard as she could. She stood up to get more leverage. Every movement she made was an attempt to go faster. It should have been impossible for her to catch up with them, but it was as if they slowed in response to her chase.

The whirring, clicking sound of a hundred bicycles edged closer and closer to her, and then she was among them.

The world went white, as if she had ridden into a cloud. Her body was still riding, still gripping the handlebars and pressing the pedals, but her mind was in a misty white freefall, hurtling closer and closer to something, something important. *Just like the Crystal Warriors in the Great Cosmic Cloud . . .*

The world popped back into place. Carly sucked in a big breath of air, as if she had been underwater and just breached the surface. She was staring at the backs of long-limbed bicycle riders, their skin gray and brown and glowing, their limbs long and in motion. She was staring at them moving farther away from her. She felt like she was being dragged backward, away from her goal. She kept pedaling as fast as she could, but it was no use. The group continued to edge away from her.

"No!" she shouted. "No, no, no, no, no, no!"

It wasn't supposed to happen like this. She'd made the leap of faith! She did everything Annabeth did! Why wasn't she able to retrieve her prize?

She stopped the bike and rested with one foot on the ground, her head hanging down to her handlebars. For the first time since she was, like, nine years old, tears welled in her eyes.

"You are a brave little thing, aren't you?"

Carly froze at the sound of the slippery, hissing voice, her tears sinking back inside her, freezing her heart with ice-cold fear.

"Did you enjoy the dream we sent you?"

"No!"

She looked up without thinking, and the sight of the grinning elfin entity before her caused her legs to fold. Her bike clattered to the street, and she scrambled backward, away from the large cyclist.

The cyclist laughed. When the group of them had laughed, the sound had seemed sinister, but now, one-on-one, Carly heard it more as a muffled tinkling sound, like bells with wads of paper shoved into them. She looked up again.

"Are you a ghost? Or a fairy?"

There was that laugh again. "You can call me a fairy if you like, little one."

This certainly wasn't the kind of fairy she'd imagined from reading *The Crystal Warriors*. Those were small, mischievous things with wings and glitter and melodious voices. The fairy in front of her loomed from where it sat on its bicycle. Its shaggy black hair was almost mane-like, pooling around its shoulders and framing its pointed, green-tinged face. Its eyes were black with no whites showing. Carly wanted to get up and run, but she knew how fast these things were. She couldn't even keep up with them, let alone outrun them.

"You brought me something nice," said the fairy. "I wanted to thank you."

A book—no, *her* book—materialized in the fairy's hand. It flipped through the pages with long fingers tipped with sharp claws.

Thinking she would receive her book back, Carly held out her hand.

The fairy gave her a look, then laughed again.

"A gift once given cannot be returned to the giver."

"I didn't *give* you anything!"

As the fairy's gaze sank into her, Carly lowered her hand. She wasn't going to get her book back. She wasn't sure she was going to get out of this at all. Maybe they would take her with them, and she'd be cursed to ride magical bikes through boring streets every year. Would her hair grow long and shaggy? Would her limbs get long and her face pointed like theirs?

A soft night breeze lifted the smell of crushed garlic to her nose, and she was struck by how real the world was. Sights, sounds, smells. Even the unearthly creature in front of her.

"We like you, little one," said the fairy. "We will return part of your gift."

It placed its hands flat on each cover of the book. Carly was worried the fairy would throw it or rip it or harm it some other way, but instead it just closed its eyes and breathed in.

Something insubstantial, like a wavy mist, rose from the book and circled the fairy's face before disappearing into its skin. A pink tinge flooded the fairy's cheeks. Its hair became almost imperceptibly smoother, less wild.

Then it threw the book right at Carly's head.

She caught it, of course. But not before the corner banged her in the temple.

"Ow!"

The fairy yawned and stretched, as if it was trying to signal that the conversation was over.

"My horde waits for me. I will go now. It was nice meeting you, Book Girl."

The creature hopped on its bicycle and began to ride away, its green glow growing brighter as it did. It had nearly disappeared down the street when Carly remembered the golf club.

"Wait! My dad's golf club! He's going to kill me."

She gripped her book. It had been returned to her. No, she had gotten it back. She was a Crystal Warrior after all. But when she opened it, skimming through the pages, she didn't feel as delighted as she should have been. The words didn't jump out at her. The names of characters didn't give her that warm glow of familiarity. She checked pages 92 and 93, but didn't see the stains she knew should be there. Maybe the light was playing tricks on her. She turned to the first page, intending to read a chapter or two before heading home, but something didn't sit quite right. After all that, the book didn't draw her in like it used to. She shoved the book in her backpack, hopped on her bike, and headed home.

The sun was rising by the time she returned her bike to the garage. Somehow, a simple conversation with the fairy had taken hours. Or maybe it was the time she'd spent riding with them. That could have gone on longer than she thought. She hated it. They shouldn't be allowed to just kidnap girls for the night, no matter how nice their bicycles are.

She crashed into bed still in her clothes. She'd barely been able to close her eyes before her mom was knocking at her door, telling her it was time to get up for school.

"Oh, and you have a package," her mom said.

"A package?" Carly's mouth was thick with dry saliva, as if she had slept after all.

"Yeah, it might be a book. Were you expecting something?"

Carly launched out of bed despite her exhaustion. She ripped the door open and grabbed the package from her mother.

It was a book, or something book-shaped, wrapped in brown paper. A note on the front read "For your bravery."

Carly shook as she peeled the paper away. Maybe this was her actual book, not the blank, lifeless copy the fairy had given her. *My book, my book, my book!*

But it was not her book. It was not *The Crystal Warriors*, book one of the Crystal Warriors series.

Her mom peered upside down at the book in Carly's hands. "An advance reader copy? Who sent you this?"

"No idea," Carly said, even though she knew exactly who'd sent it. "Mom, can I skip school today?"

"Absolutely not."

"Please!"

"No, I will not have you missing your entire life because your head is stuck in a book."

She'd never understand. This wasn't just any book. It was an advance copy of *The Crystal Warriors: Curse of the Dragon Pearl*. It wasn't even out yet!

"Fine, I'll go. But can I have a new bicycle?"

Her mother stared at her, incredulous. "You want a bicycle?"

"Yeah. Maybe I'll, you know, get out more or whatever."

Her mother threw up her hands before scooping Carly into a hug. "I will never understand this child."

"But you will give her a new bike?" Carly asked.

"Maybe Santa will come early."

Carly rolled her eyes. She knew Santa wasn't real. Everyone knew that.

"Hey honey?" called Carly's dad from the garage door. He was holding his golf bag. "Have you seen my nine iron?"

Carly took advantage of the distraction by retreating back into her room. Why had she even cared so much about one specific copy of a book? As long as she did her chores and got her allowance, she could get a new one from the bookstore whenever she wanted!

She changed into school clothes, wolfed down breakfast, brushed her teeth, and headed out the door.

With a whispered *thank you*, Carly left through the front door and made her way to her bus stop. As she walked, she cracked open her new book.

THE HELLSTREAM EXPEDITION
∽ *Cara Brezina* ∽

"*A* bicycle?" Mitzi repeated in horror. "You bought a *bicycle*?"

Her dismayed reaction was drowned out by the excited and astonished exclamations of the rest of the Sariah Society gathered in the university canteen.

"Where'd you get it?"

"Can we see it?"

"Have you ridden it yet?"

"When can we try it out?"

Chantal basked in their enthusiasm, a hint of a smug smile quirking at her lips. At last, she gave in and held up an image on her phone. For Chantal, it was the equivalent of hoisting a banner and dancing on the table.

"It's an exact replica of Sariah's original bicycle."

"Wo-o-o-w!"

The young women crowded around the tiny photo, familiar to them from a handful of bicycle images from the group's Sariah archives. The conveyance would more accurately have been described as a tricycle, but since Sariah had always called hers a bicycle, the Sariah Society had never questioned the terminology. The vehicle had a fat front tire that was slightly higher than the two back tires. A tall pole behind the seat held up a device that functioned as a combination wind turbine and stabilization rudder. The designers had included the feature as an adaptation to Winken-B's low gravity and fierce winds, but the result had not been particularly effective. Bicycles never gained a following on the planet.

"There's actually a lot of interest in historical vehicles used in early colonization programs," Chantal was saying. "I found a salvage company that can assemble customized vehicles from their inventory, as long as none of the components are rare. I obtained a list of parts used in Sariah's bicycle, and they were able to put together a replica for me."

"Have you tested it?" broke in Grete, a cultural studies major at Winken-B West Grove University. If Mitzi had dared to interrupt, her immediate concern would have been, *Is it remotely legal to ride the thing?*

Chantal disregarded the question, which conveyed a firm no to everyone in the group. She pushed her food tray to the side and drew a large digital tablet out of her satchel. She reserved this device exclusively for Sariah Society matters, and it served mainly as the repository of her copy of *Discourse, Ephemera, and Reminiscence*, the gigantic semi-autobiographical scrapbook that Sariah had released shortly before her death.

"In the *DER*, Sariah wrote that for her inaugural trip on the bicycle, she rose at dawn, conveyed the bicycle to Aolian Hill, which was on the outskirts of the city back then, and spent the morning pedaling through the Aolian Grove."

"Not a chance," Hylda put in. "Everybody who knew Sariah says that she was never up at dawn. She liked to depict the rising suns in her artwork, that's why she was always claiming that she was out and about at dawn."

"Regardless," Chantal said, raising her voice slightly. "I wasn't going to suggest that we try to recreate Sariah's original first ride. The Aolian Grove is much too congested nowadays. I was thinking that we could meet tomorrow morning at the Kell Nature Preserve. It doesn't attract that many visitors, and the terrain is flat and even. We should be able to master the bicycle without much trouble and then it's onward to the Hellstream Highway for the Sariah Society."

"But not at dawn," Grete stated, without bothering to make it sound like a question.

Chantal had pursed her lips in disapproval at Grete cutting off her rallying cry.

"Midmorning should be fine. Incidentally, there are still a couple fine details to finalize on the bike before it will be fully functional. Brakes, and stuff. No big deal."

Despair had led Mitzi to the Sariah Society. During her second year at the university, she'd fallen into a despondency that she couldn't understand or shake off. It had descended without incitement and without warning. She found herself in the therapist's office apologizing for wasting the woman's time, being as she couldn't even describe a specific cause of her malaise. The therapist assured her that her condition was completely normal, although not so normal that Mitzi didn't need help.

Try meditation, exercise, journaling, joining a club, or taking up a hobby, the therapist had intoned. Mitzi had tentatively mentioned that she'd once enjoyed drawing, and the therapist had pounced in triumph. *Your assignment before the next session: obtain drawing materials.*

So, Mitzi had found herself staring at a blank drawing pad and experiencing an utter lack of inspiration. She decided that maybe it would help to explore some of the subjects that had attracted notable Winkenden artists.

The gallery display she brought up on her phone had included a multimedia landscape by Sariah Zee, and the images had been a revelation for Mitzi. A few weeks later, when she saw a flyer in the university's art building advertising a meeting of the Sariah Society, she'd snapped a photo of the date and time, returning to it over and again before deciding an hour beforehand that she wasn't going to attend. Five minutes before the meeting was set to begin, she rushed out of her dorm room and was only a couple minutes late.

She'd thought that she'd find herself surrounded by art lovers, but it turned out, at least according to Chantal, that Sariah was also known as a renowned naturalist, philosopher, musician, poet, and cultural critic. The only other club member who was deeply familiar with her artwork immediately started talking about the debate over

Sariah's perceived status as an outsider artist. Beryl's side of the conversation practically contained footnotes.

Mitzi found a greater resonance with Hylda and her bandmates in the Smirking Minervas, all of whom were club members. Hylda had asked her why she was interested in Sariah, and Mitzi haltingly told her how she'd been struck by the sense of joy in Sariah's artwork. She wasn't sure whether the pieces depicted fantastical landscapes or psychedelic hallucinations—there had been scholarly arguments in both camps, as well as many others—but she did know that the bold color contrasts and dizzying designs made her feel happy at a time when everything else in the world seemed to exists in shades of drabness.

Hylda had nodded agreement as if this made complete sense to her. She'd first encountered the name Sariah Zee in the footnote of a music history book that described her as experimental and provocative. Upon listening to the albums, Hylda had found the songs fun and subversive, and fiendishly clever.

At her next therapy session, Mitzi showed her therapist a few sketches of landscapes and abstract designs inspired by Sariah's art. In the weeks that followed, she found herself bringing up Sariah's music and poetry and her short, dynamic life. She also started talking about her new associates, as she thought of the Sariah Society. She'd begun to dare to think of them as friends in the back of her mind, but she didn't yet feel confident saying the word out loud. Her therapist didn't push her on the matter, either.

Things were trending up with her involvement in the Sariah Society. New interests, new friends, fun intellectual wrangling. But Mitzi hadn't reckoned on the bicycle.

Mitzi spent most of the morning inventing excuses accounting for her absence at the Kell Nature Preserve. She ultimately failed in finding an adequate one and arrived about a half hour later than the appointed time. Unsurprisingly, none of the members of the Sariah Society had yet mounted the bicycle by the time she sidled up to the back of the group. They were the only other people she'd seen in the Kell Nature Preserve.

On most planets, a nature preserve on the outskirts of a major city would be a significant attraction. But on Winken-B, establishing a nature preserve on land owned by the planetary government was like setting up a bake sale stand inside a cake shop. Winken-B was known for only one reason: the towering swaths of kintl trees that covered much of the planet, forming patterns visible from space as weblike networks. Tourists loved the effect, and transport shuttles usually devoted an hour to an aerial tour of the surface as they gradually descended.

And lots of tourists descended. The kintl trees were taller than skyscrapers and unique among all forms of native planetary life. They resembled huge ferns or grasses more than trees, and their biology was closer to that of fungi than plants, but they had been dubbed trees by the first explorers and the name stuck. Most of the planet's surface was conserved as a protected environment.

Not a single kintl tree stood within the borders of the Kell Nature Preserve, although the treeline of the nearest swath was visible off to the northeast. The preserve had been established to highlight the biome known as midline prairie.

It wasn't a huge draw for tourists. But there was some great terrain for cycling, according to Chantal, not least because of the lack of potential victims primed to jump in the path of the bicycle.

Chantal caught sight of Mitzi and gave a big smile.

"We're ready to roll!" she announced.

Nobody made a move to mount the bicycle. Mitzi noticed that the members of the Smirking Minervas were carrying their tool kits. They were adept in tinkering with mechanical and electronic gear from their experience working with musical instruments and sound equipment.

"The bike's working?" Mitzi asked.

Hylda shrugged.

"We got the wheels to go around. What more would you ask?"

"There was no guarantee for Sariah, either," Chantal assured them. "Who wants to go first?"

Mitzi wasn't fooled by her broad smile and upbeat tone. Chantal was almost as scared of the bike as she was.

There was no shortage of volunteers, and the winner was Dalia, a philosophy major who also played rugby. She mounted the bike seat and set her feet on the pedals.

"Ready, set, go!" the Sariah Society chanted in unison.

Dalia began pedaling, and, for a moment, the bike was a vision of tricyclic fleetness and grace. For at least ten seconds, before the front wheel slewed off to the right and the bicycle skidded to the left. Managing to stay on the seat, she looked back to whoop in triumph. As she raised a fist over her head, the bike slewed to the right on the uneven surface and Dalia toppled to the ground before she could return both hands to the handlebars.

The Sariah Society sprinted in solidarity to their fallen comrade, but Dalia was already on her feet and checking herself for damage by the time they joined her.

"I'm fine," she told them. "How's the bike?"

"Bike's fine," Hylda said. "As long as you don't take a hammer to it, that thing will keep functioning."

"Someone will probably try that before the end of the day," Grete added.

"We haven't yet seen any proof of the functioning, either," another of the Smirking Minervas put in.

"It was a solid first effort," Chantal said, her voice carrying over the commentary. "Contemporary accounts indicated that the rider had to keep a firm grip on the handles, otherwise any irregularity on the ground would cause the front wheel to deflect."

"The bike caught me by surprise when the wheel turned on a stone," Dalia said. "You don't have to have heroic upper body strength to manage the thing. As long as you stay vigilant, you should manage to keep upright."

"Any volunteers?" Chantal asked.

Nobody had been dissuaded by witnessing Dalia's spill, and the next bike rider managed fourfold Dalia's distance before toppling over. Once again, the Sariah Society raced to her side.

"Are you okay?" Chantal puffed.

"That was great!" came the reply.

By midafternoon, the Sariah Society had mastered bicycle riding, and Mitzi had gotten the most exercise of her lifetime chasing after the bicyclists. Eventually, she gave up following the bicycle and retreated to the visitor center, where she rented a hover scooter and bought a case of drinks. When she returned to the trail, the Sariah Society was exuberantly grateful for the hydration. Nobody razzed her about the scooter, either. Not while they were all guzzling the drinks she'd provided.

"Have you had a turn yet?" Hylda finally asked. Mitzi cringed back, but it wasn't necessary. Hylda was directing the question to Chantal.

"I wanted to give everyone else a chance first," Chantal said with an unconvincing, deprecating laugh. "Of course I'm eager to finally have the opportunity to ride the bike."

She wasn't quite quivering with fear, and nobody expressed any doubts about her enthusiasm and courage. The Sariah Society members solicitously helped her onto the seat and clustered around until she announced that she was ready to start pedaling. They released their hold on the handles and various other parts of the bike, and Chantal's body, and her ride, were underway.

"Mind if I borrow your scooter?" Dalia asked Mitzi a few seconds after Chantal had begun her wobbly progress down the plain. Mitzi assented, and Dalia accelerated forward to trail Chantal at a polite distance.

The measure of caution turned out to be unnecessary. Before long, the bike lurched as Chantal encountered a stretch of loose stone, but she applied the brakes and kept a firm grip on the handles. The bike slowed to a wobble and the Sariah Society applauded.

Chantal graciously ceded the bike to Dalia for the final ride back to the transit station.

"You didn't get a chance to ride, Mitzi," Hylda said as they retraced their steps. "Want to give the bicycle a quick spin? We've got plenty of time."

Mitzi assured Hylda that she was too exhausted to embark on a ride after such an active day. That much was the truth.

♤ • ♧

It had taken a little while for Mitzi to realize that Sariah Zee was less than universally adored and venerated. Winken-B tourist blurbs sometimes described her as a "personality" or the neutral "society figure." She was remembered more for her stunts than her creative and intellectual output. It was not unheard of for her to be referred to as a "crackpot" or "crank."

Most of the Sariah Society was unbothered by the lack of universal respect for their guiding light, and some of the members delighted in her inconsistent reputation.

"I mean, why can't she be recognized as both whimsical and serious at the same time?" Hylda had once said to Mitzi. "I think that some people resent her simply because she's impossible to categorize. And yeah, as much as Chantal would prefer to downplay it, she was an exhibitionist, and some of her stunts were downright brilliant. Did you ever watch the footage of her Promenade of Ubiquitous Perturbations? You really should. Anyway, there's no reason you can't appreciate that side of her but still recognize her as a philosopher and naturalist, et cetera, et cetera."

Chantal took a darker view on prevailing attitudes regarding Sariah, though she veered between considering anything short of universal acclaim a result of either an elitist hatchet job or anti-intellectual conspiracy. Either way, she also blamed laziness on the part of historians who should have been more diligent in documenting key points in Winken-B history.

She had a very specific event in mind.

From the moment of its discovery, Winken-B had been renowned for the vast kintl trees towering high above the ground. It had taken a couple centuries for biologists to discover that the realm of the towering kintl trees extended below the ground. Certain types of roots exuded compounds that eroded soil and stone and promoted the growth of microbes that further ate away their surroundings. Over the course of thousands of years, each kintl tree created a network of connected underground chambers nestled here and there inside its vast root mass.

Dr. Arvin Sedge had described the caverns as a tree nursery in suspension, providing a protected environment for young shoots to imbibe nutrients. If the parent tree were killed, the youngsters could quickly emerge from the soil. This early rapid growth spurt, combined with the sheer number of potential successors rising from the roots, increased the odds that at least one of the saplings would survive the pests that would immediately descend on the delicate shoots.

Dr. Sedge had discovered the first of the kintl caves and determined their role in the kintl reproductive cycle. He'd talked about his experiences and scientific legacy when receiving the Winken-B Certificate of Merit, the planet's highest honor, for his work. In his acceptance speech, he'd thanked Sariah Zee, saying that he owed her for setting him on the path toward understanding the nature of kintl trees.

Nobody had taken him literally, of course. Maybe she'd served as an inspiration, some said. The less generous claimed that he was being overly sentimental, or that he'd been pandering to the younger generation.

Chantal took him at his word. One of the collages in Sariah's *Discourse, Ephemera, and Reminiscence* depicted a darkly crosshatched chamber that could, arguably, be interpreted as a kintl cavern. It had been created several months before Dr. Sedge's exploration of the first kintl cave. Chantal had linked the artwork to an epic bicycle ride that Sariah had taken on the Hellstream Highway.

The Hellstream Plain was the site of one of Winken-B's great natural disasters. About 20,000 years ago, a flood of sulphuric acid had inundated a lowland plain of kintl trees, killing the entire grove. The deluge had long since receded, leaving behind a dead and barren wasteland.

Tourists didn't flock to the Hellstream Highway, as the central riverbed had been dubbed, but Sariah thought that it would be an ideal site to build up some speed on her bicycle. She'd ridden like the devil down the dry waterway, danced on the hot, caked earth, had a picnic on a ridge that had been formed from a downed kintl tree, and seen some *amazing* sights.

That was the crux of the conundrum, in Chantal's view. Did those *amazing* sights include a cavern below one the kintl stumps, perhaps collapsed or broken open in the aftermath of the ecological disaster?

They'd obtained the bicycle. Now, the Sariah Society was going to recreate Sariah's historic ride and investigate whether those *amazing* sights could have included a kintl cave.

It transpired that the Hellstream Highway expedition would be a test of the Sariah Society's finances as well as fortitude. Chantal's expression grew progressively more dour as she reported on the cost of shuttle bus tickets to the Itoian Event Area, as the Hellstream Plain was officially designated, and then on the transport fees for the bicycle. The trip was going to clean out the group's budget for the school year. Several members volunteered to pay their own fares, but Chantal declared that it would be inconsistent with Sariah's egalitarian ideals. The Smirking Minervas pledged that they could repair any issues with the bicycle using parts scrounged from the Robotics/AI Club's trash. Chantal did not appear reassured.

Mitzi offered to stay behind, but her suggestion was firmly refused as well.

After much planning, bickering, packing, grandstanding, and jouncing in an antiquated shuttle bus for three hours, the Sariah Society stood at the gateway to the Hellstream Plain. There was no actual structural gateway, only a sign indicating the demarcation between two different protected chunks of land. Not many tourists visited the site, and few scientists had studied the graveyard of the ruined kintl forest. The government preferred to allocate funding to projects focusing on living specimens.

The Sariah Society hadn't bothered checking the weather forecast for their chosen date. Every day on the Hellstream Plain was sunny, chilly, and bone dry.

After the shuttle dropped them off and unloaded the bicycle, the members of the Sariah Society stood on the slight rise next to the sign and goggled at the landscape. From above, most of the surface of Winken-B was lush and verdant. The Hellstream Plain was an insult, a seething reddish gash cut into the green velvet. From the ground, Mitzi saw an undulating plain without a single leaf of vegetative growth. The horizon appeared fuzzy, the sky above the straight line of ground gradually changing from dusty rose to the usual clear teal overhead.

Chantal's eyes were on the slight dip directly ahead of them. It didn't much resemble a highway.

"Let's go. Onward to the Hellsteam Highway."

They'd drawn lots for the honor of being the first rider, and Dalia had nabbed the spot once again. She'd immediately offered to forfeit, but the Sariah Society had seen her selection as a good omen.

The Smirking Minervas gave the bicycle a quick examination to check that it had not been damaged in transit. With their sanction, Chantal ceremonially rolled it into place next to the marker sign. She brought up a page of the *DER* onto her tablet.

"I rose at dawn," she intoned. Someone snorted. Chantal paused as she skimmed ahead. "I wended my way to the infernal Hellstream Plain, putting my faith in my trusty bicycle. . . . For twenty minutes, I pedaled like a demon until spying some intriguing features in this desolate landscape to explore."

Chantal switched to the stopwatch function.

"Are you ready?"

The Sariah Society answered for Dalia with a chorus of cheers.

"And, go!"

Dalia leaned forward as she began pedaling, giving her best impression of a modern-day demon. The rest of the Sariah Society brought out their folding hover scooters borrowed from the campus tour center, a strategy they'd adopted after Mitzi's scooter rental on that first bicycle day. They would follow in a squadron and explore the area surrounding Dalia's stopping point.

Unfortunately, Sariah had not made any note of the total distance she'd traveled in those twenty minutes. While the rest of the Society surveyed the locale, Dalia would pedal the bike back to the starting point, along with another member who would perform the next ride. The group would repeat the process at her stopping point. Chantal was confident that one of the trips would yield the "intriguing features" where Sariah had seen those "*amazing* sights."

Dalia came to a stop after bicycling seventeen kilometers. There were no geographical features in the vicinity, intriguing or otherwise.

"Let's spread out in all directions, to a distance of a kilometer or a bit more," Chantal directed the group. "There might be points of interest here that aren't immediately obvious."

Mitzi veered to the right and reduced the speed of her scooter to a fast walking pace. She mostly kept her eyes on the ground as she moved along, hunting for signs of a hidden cavern. Occasionally, she brought out her binoculars and scanned in the distance for interesting features, or any sort of features at all. By the time the Sariah Society members delivered the unanimous report that they'd found nothing noteworthy, the next rider had come to a stop after bicycling more than nineteen kilometers. The group accelerated their scooters forward to the next reconnaissance site.

A few hours later, morale was flagging. Most of the riders managed between fifteen and twenty kilometers, and they'd surveyed the area surrounding that stretch of the Hellstream Highway quite thoroughly.

"How did she manage to find intriguing features after twenty minutes on her first try?" one of the Smirking Minervas groused.

"Sariah's mind was receptive to the unique marvels of this environment," Hylda said, straight-faced. Mitzi tried to figure out whether she was being sarcastic.

Chantal announced that everyone would feel better after rest and sustenance. Half of the group could take a lunch break during the next ride, the other half during the ride after that.

The next rider up was Hylda, and she managed a distance of nearly twenty-three kilometers. The half of the Society who was settling down to eat directed enthusiastic words of encouragement to the bedraggled half who began wending their way toward Hylda. They no longer resembled a squadron.

At Hylda's stopping point, the Hellstream Highway was bisected by one of the ridges created by the fallen kintl trees, although the rare flash floods had evened out the riverbed terrain over the eons. The members of the Sariah Society split up and followed the course of the trunk a couple kilometers in either direction. They found a couple sites where branches forked away from the main rise, but there were no indications of cavities beneath ground level.

Chantal rode late in the day, and the group's flagging spirits briefly rose in hope. She managed a respectable fifteen kilometers, coming to a halt at a point in the road that had already been thoroughly explored by the Sariah Society. The rider that followed also managed a familiar eighteen kilometers. Some of the members of the group didn't bother standing up until being prodded by a glare from Chantal.

She gazed around as if she half expected a hole leading underground to suddenly open up off to the side of the Hellstream Highway. Everyone avoided her eyes, not wanting to witness the exact moment that she gave up on the improbable dream.

Chantal wasn't quite ready to capitulate.

"Mitzi! You haven't done your ride yet, have you?"

"Huh? Wha?"

Mitzi froze. It had seemed that the Society had largely accepted her as mascot rather than active participant in this endeavor, and she had almost relinquished her fear of being coaxed onto the bike. But the group happily transferred its attention from Chantal to her.

"You'll feel a real sense of accomplishment afterwards," Hylda assured her.

The entire membership of the Sariah Society accompanied her back to the starting point, which didn't convey much optimism that the trip would prove a success. Mitzi tried to object that she didn't want to waste their time. They solicitously and ruthlessly assured her that they wouldn't dream of depriving her of the opportunity.

A dozen capable hands helped her position herself on the bike's seat and then withdrew. The bike wobbled.

"Maybe we should hold onto the handlebars until she's got some momentum?" Grete suggested.

"We can't do that," Chantal said regretfully. "It wouldn't be historically authentic if we helped out."

"Are you ready for us to disengage the auxiliary brake?" Grete asked Mitzi.

Nope. Never.

"All ready," Mitzi said.

The bicycle rolled gently down the slight incline, then suddenly gathered velocity and almost accelerated out of Mitzi's control. She remembered the lessons about keeping a firm grip on the handlebars and clenched her fists tight, locking her wrists and elbows into place. She felt like she had to pedal fast to keep up with the bicycle's speed, not generate it.

The bicycle slowed as the slope leveled off, and pedaling suddenly required an effort. Mitzi did not feel like she was pedaling like a demon. She felt more like she was trudging through thick mud. Her knees and thighs protested the unreasonable demands of the bicycle.

She glanced at the small screen in the center of the handlebars to check her time. She'd been bicycling for just seven minutes. The front wheel attempted to set its own course off to the left, and she tightened her hold to keep the bicycle on the Hellstream Highway. A small part of her mind suggested that if she were to topple over, it would provide a quick end to the ordeal.

Mitzi banished the notion.

By the time her twenty minutes were nearly elapsed, she felt like she was pedaling through a half-waking nightmare. Voices called to her from the edges of her consciousness.

"You did it! Time's up, Mitzi! Great job!"

She would have fallen off the bicycle, but the Sariah Society was already surrounding her and easing her to the ground.

"Almost thirteen kilometers," Chantal told her. "That's . . . really something."

"And we have some new terrain to explore!" Grete declared.

Later on, Mitzi could recall the aftermath of her ride only in a series of discrete moments. Hylda calling out that a tall outcrop appeared to be the remnants of a kintl stump. Another member screaming that she'd found the remnants of a sinkhole. A queue of Sariah Society members disappearing into a crevice at one side of the sinkhole, all wearing safety helmets equipped with spotlights and carrying ropes, which proved to be unnecessary. A few minutes later, Chantal's voice, screeching out, "Don't touch it! Don't touch it!"

The small group who had stayed behind stood rigid, their hands ready to summon emergency services on their devices. Before long, one of the Smirking Minervas emerged from the darkness.

"It's a glove! We found one of Sariah's gloves that she dropped inside the cave!"

That night, the Sariah Society checked into a hotel in the nearest tourist resort enclave. The Smirking Minervas volunteered to foot the bill from their treasury. Chantal graciously accepted the offer with an airy promise of repayment from the grants that would undoubtedly be inundating the Society following the historic discovery.

The group crowded into two hotel rooms, with Sariah Society members draped across every soft piece of furniture and covering most of the rug. Everyone insisted that Mitzi take a space on one of the beds, even though she told them that she'd sleep just as well on the tile floor.

Before dropping off, Mitzi thought back to her initial exploration of Sariah's works in the cool, quiet, orderly atmosphere of the school library. Now, she was surrounded by a chaotic scrum of ecstatic, unwashed young women, all bound together by their personal connection to Sariah. And to each other.

Not long ago, she would have been terrified by such a prospect.

The next day, the Society returned to the Hellstream Highway, this time accompanied by faculty from the Winken-B West Forest University history and planetary science departments as well as a reporter from the region's media outlet, the West Grove Vine. It took them less than ten minutes to reach the site.

"Sariah really didn't make it very far on her bike, did she?" Chantal said, softly enough that only a few members of the Society could hear.

"She was a visionary, not an athlete," Hylda assured her.

The three outsiders initially appeared bemused by Chantal's extravagant claims, but their interest sharpened as they stepped into the cavern. Lights reflected off of the softly rounded, glassy jet-black walls, and the geologist speculated that the unusual rock had been formed by microbial agents reacting with the toxic floodwaters. The historian, who was also a curator at the West Grove Museum of Natural Science, imaged the glove with a portable scanner and brought up a view of the material. After a short examination, she pronounced it a historical artifact displaying notable deterioration. Grete showed her a page in the *DER* showing Sariah wearing identical gloves with the ornately stitched letter *S* on each hand. The historian agreed that the resemblance was worth further investigation.

"Sariah? Wasn't she some colonization-era socialite?" the reporter asked upon hearing the name. Chantal narrowed her eyes and volunteered to clarify the nature of Sariah's contributions to Winken-B civilization. The litany did not cease until everyone exited the cave single file.

✍ • ✍

A few days after returning from the expedition, the Sariah Society gathered in the canteen to celebrate their triumph. The mood was euphoric as everyone munched on snacks and retold their greatest Hellstream Highway moments.

"After all, we deserve to sit back and relax and bask in our glory for a while, don't we?" Hylda said.

The words made complete sense, but Mitzi thought she detected a slightly sardonic note in Hylda's voice.

"What do you mean?" Mitzi asked.

"Wait for it."

Hylda nodded toward the table where Chantal had just stood to share a few words with the Society. The group leader was glowing. They'd all been featured as the main story on the *Winken-B West Grove University Courier*, though Grete had shared her suspicion that the honor was mainly due to the novelty of the outlandish bicycle at the center of the group picture. Chantal raised a glass and beamed at them.

"Ladies, we have so much work to do!"

DOWN MEMORY LANE
✍ *Lisa Timpf* ✍

A door chime sounded, low and musical, as I stepped through the front entry of the Jarcoe Public Library. I paused to survey my surroundings, mouth slightly open. *Wow. Things sure have changed since the last time I was in here.*

"Hi, Mandy. Haven't seen you in a while. Are you looking for something?" A tall woman wearing a blue and grey library staff golf shirt offered a welcoming smile.

She seems to know me, but I don't . . . I frowned, trying to put a name to a face as the woman drew closer. Then I noticed her name tag. *Sheryl Lever.*

Memory flooded back. Standing in the face-off circle, that championship game ten years ago, and locking my gaze with hers, just for a few seconds, before focusing on the puck drop.

The memory made me grimace. Sheryl and her teammates had been our bitter rivals in ice hockey and softball, right up to the day I reluctantly hung up my skates and cleats, but that's not what caused the change in facial expression. No; recalling that staredown in the face-off circle reminded me of who had been standing to my right, waiting for the puck to spring loose. Allie. Since the first team we played on together, we'd always been side by side.

And we never will be again.

Don't think about that. Keep your pain to yourself. Nobody else wants to hear about it.

Showing emotions left you vulnerable. I'd learned that, working in a male-dominated organization, where any show of compassion, empathy, or sensitivity got labelled as a sign of weakness. I hadn't allowed myself to be vulnerable for years. *Except with Allie. And after she died . . .*

That particular train of thought, I didn't care to board.

I forced a smile. "I didn't know you were a librarian," I said. It wasn't particularly articulate, but it was the first thing that popped into my head.

"Information technologist, Class II," Sheryl replied. She shrugged. "Second career."

"Still playing hockey?" I asked her, trying to keep an envious edge from my voice.

"Nope. Gave it up in '32." Sheryl smiled. "But I'm assuming you didn't come here to quiz me up on my sports involvement."

"I didn't. I was looking for something." I leaned to my left, trying to see past her. "It's been a while since I've visited the library. It looks—different."

"It is different." Sheryl nodded. "In the years after the First Pandemic, we moved to online delivery for many of our offerings. Phased out most of our paper-and-ink books."

"Then what—"

"What do we offer? There're still some people who want to do research on original materials that we have on zip-film—because of copyright, we can't just put that out on the 'net. We offer workstations for people who don't have e-book readers at home. And we maintain a physical repository of audiobooks and audio-vids."

I nodded. "A disc-case is easier to sanitize than the pages of a book."

"You've got it."

"That's what I'm looking for, actually," I said. "Audio-vids for exercise. I have the one that came with the bike, but I've pretty much worn it out."

Sheryl arched an eyebrow. "You've got a synch-bike?"

"Dyna-Pedal," I said.

Sheryl nodded. "I've been thinking of getting one myself. Between the smog ratings and the heat we've had this summer, that's a safer way to stay fit than pedaling around town. I'll show you where the discs are displayed, and leave you to it." She led the way toward a series of racks to my left.

The library's audio-vid selection proved impressive, vindicating my choice to leave the comfort of home and venture out into society—something I'd avoided since Allie's death, aside from essential trips to the grocery store and the pharmacy.

If it'd been me who went first, Allie would have gotten back out there. She always was better at moving on from things.

But I'm not Allie.

After selecting an audio-vid set in Halifax, I turned to look for Sheryl, so I could thank her for her assistance. But she'd disappeared into the labyrinthine back section of the library. To my surprise, I experienced a pang of regret. She was a link to the past, in a present that often left me feeling unmoored.

You haven't been out in a while, that's all, I told myself. *Don't let yourself get soft now. That doesn't lead anywhere good.*

I wandered over to the self-checkout, scanned my card and the audio-vid, and departed.

✐ • ✎

Though the basement of my small bungalow maintained a cooler temperature than the main floor, sweat beaded on my forehead and arms as I pedaled my bike up a long, steep hill. Or appeared to do so. My Dyna-Pedal's program synched with the audio-vid player to increase and decrease resistance depending on the terrain. Between the scenery playing on the big-screen TV in front of me and the audio patter, which included narration and background noises, it was easy to sustain the illusion that my ride had taken me somewhere other than a slightly musty rec room.

The screen also had a banner-style readout providing the calorie count, time spent, and interval remaining to the next difficulty level change.

The Halifax Citadel loomed ahead. *Maybe I'll take a break and have a look around when I get there,* I told myself.

I'd chosen Halifax for my first borrowed audio-vid because it was familiar, yet safe. I'd attended grad school at Dalhousie right after undergrad, so it was before I met Allie.

Six months had passed since Allie's death, as a result of a mutated form of Ebola scything through the world's population, and I thought I was doing well dealing with the loss. Still, I didn't go around seeking reminders of our time together.

In the early days after her death, I'd succumbed to a serious bout of the blues, constantly thinking of all the little things I should have done differently. Haunted by the feeling that I didn't appreciate our time together while we had it. That I'd let life sift through my fingers, like sand at the beach. Sleep often proved elusive, and I'd learned through experience that a hard workout during the day helped. I leaned into the hill climb, listening intently to the audio description of the labour and ingenuity that went into constructing the Citadel back in the mid-1800s.

When I reached the top of the hill, I checked the metrics and grinned. Engrossed in the scenery, I'd beaten my previous best workout time, and the calorie consumption estimate read gratifyingly high.

Point Pleasant Park tomorrow, I promised myself. *Or maybe I'll check out that segment on the history of Halifax's universities.*

Which would include Dalhousie and all of its attendant memories.

I waited to see if that notion would invoke a stab of nostalgia, and breathed a sigh of relief. Nope, that far back, I was safe. I'd best stick with it.

༄ • ༅

"How's it going?" Whether by design or chance, once again, it was Sheryl who greeted me at the library entrance six weeks later. "The simulations are pretty great, right?"

"Very immersive," I said. "You feel as though you're actually there."

"Hey, I meant to ask last time, but how's Allie?"

"Died in 2034. Complications from the Ebola virus."

"I'm so sorry," Sheryl said. The color drained from her cheeks.

I shrugged. "It was a while ago. I'm coping."

"I always liked her sense of humor," Sheryl said, her voice soft. "Listen, I've been keeping an eye out for you. Wanted to let you know we received a new shipment of audio-vids."

"Yeah?" Though I kept my tone neutral, I followed Sheryl toward the audio-vid racks with a rising sense of anticipation.

"I tried one of them myself. Real pretty countryside, right here in Ontario," Sheryl said. "Up in Dufferin County. You familiar with it?"

I was glad Sheryl, who had her back turned at the moment, couldn't see my face. I knew Dufferin County, all right. Allie and I had spent some of the happiest years of our life there, living on a 50-acre property that backed onto the Dufferin County Forest.

Mistaking the cause of my hesitance, Sheryl turned toward me and waved her hand. "It's pretty hilly up there. Maybe you'll want to save that until you've worked up your resistance. There's plenty of other good stuff to choose from. Like this one of the Cabot Trail, right here. Or Gaspesia, in Quebec. Come to think of it, those might be a challenge, too. Hmmm—"

I shouldn't, I told myself. I closed my eyes for a moment, swaying slightly forward.

"You okay?" Sheryl's tone conveyed genuine concern. For a moment, I felt tempted to take that as an invitation to open up. To talk to someone—anyone—about my feelings.

You know where that leads.

I clenched my jaw and looked around, doing my best to affect a casual air. "I'm fine."

Just for a moment, Sheryl's expression conveyed doubt. She hesitated, as though weighing her words.

The door chime sounded and Sheryl shot a look at the front entry, where a blond woman stood, her befuddled expression conveying a need for assistance. When no other golf-shirted workers emerged from the back area, Sheryl gestured toward the newly arrived patron. "I have to go. You know the procedure." She shot me an apologetic smile, then walked toward the newcomer, covering the ground with long strides.

I studied the audio-vid rack far longer than it should have taken to make a simple decision. Then, with trembling hands, I reached out for the *History of Dufferin County* disc.

Worst case, you can just bring it back, I assured myself. Not realizing that wasn't the worst case at all.

✍ • ✍

On each of the first two days with the new audio-vid, I set new records for exercise duration and calories burned. Best of all, I exhausted myself sufficiently to ensure a good night's sleep.

On the third day, I climbed onto the bike, eager for a strenuous workout. Picking a chapter at random, I began to pedal, finding myself on a dirt and gravel road. The Dyna-Pedal simulated the road's surface irregularities with almost painful realism, vibration passing through the handlebars and up my forearms. Only half-listening to the narrator's patter, I admired the roadside trees— poplars, pines, oaks, maples.

Then I rounded a corner, and frowned. *This looks so familiar—*

I shot a look at the green and white emergency number at the base of the driveway I was approaching, and stopped pedaling, feeling a sense of vertigo.

That's the driveway leading to our old place.

I knew the simulations would sometimes go onto private property. For example, on one particular audio-vid produced locally a few years back, you could ride through town touring the gardens of people who'd entered the Blooming Beautiful horticultural challenge.

But the people who'd owned the property after us—I wasn't sure they would have given their permission. *They liked their privacy. They likely didn't want cam-drones zipping around the property.*

Then again, the drones were incredibly discreet and unintrusive, behaving like tiny dragonflies save for their regimented flight pattern. It wouldn't be such a big deal . . .

I rode to the base of the driveway and looked upward. The long, winding gravel roadway disappeared around a bend, but I knew what lay hidden. A clearing. A stone-fronted bungalow. Outbuildings.

I wonder if everything's still the same?

I drew a breath, turned the handlebars to the right, and pedaled. I'd know pretty quickly whether the audio-vid covered this territory.

I held my breath, then released it when the narration continued without interruption, giving the history of the property and how it had been a farm back in the early 1900s. The early settlers, after investing years of back-breaking work to clear the land, struggled to make a go of farming the sandy soil. Eventually, they abandoned the enterprise and moved into a nearby town to seek work.

The people who purchased the land next took advantage of government grants and reforested the property with the white pines and red oaks native to the area.

Though I found the story interesting, I ignored the narrator when I reached the clearing where the house stood. I'd become too engrossed in comparing past and present along my own time line. The house, with its inviting front porch, still looked great. All of the outbuildings looked in decent shape. The new owners had added a shed near the garden area, as well as a fenced enclosure for some kind of livestock or pet. The enclosure appeared to be empty, for the moment at least.

Good. Nobody to raise the alarm. I shook my head. *Don't be silly. You're not really here.*

But my surroundings felt so authentic it was easy to forget that.

A managed forest logging years before we'd moved in had resulted in a number of serviceable pathways crisscrossing the property. I chose the western loop and pedaled along it, then swung back along the eastern path.

After several circuits of the property, I powered the Dyna-Pedal down. Then I trudged up the stairs, muscles weary from a good workout.

∽ • ∾

That night, I dreamed that Allie and I were still living on our rural acreage. When I awoke the next morning, I lost my sense of place, thinking I was still in our bedroom that faced south toward the forest.

The realization of where I really was, and who I was not with, came crashing down when I looked out the window.

Why did we move, anyway?

I knew the answer.

As we aged, we found the large property too much work. Besides, I'd been afraid that the housing market would collapse and we wouldn't get our money out of it when the time came to move.

We lived in paradise, and we didn't appreciate it.

Not entirely true. I had loved it when we lived there. I'd soaked in some of the moments, leaving memories ingrained. Walking an uphill path through the woods on an early spring day with sun slanting through the young leaves of the maples, rendering them an impossibly bright yellow-green. Swishing through the leaves in the fall, with our border collie Bandit bounding along the path ahead of me. Taking my prework morning walk and drinking in the pure, sweet air.

Those were the days.

As I stumbled into the kitchen to prepare breakfast, I mused that everything had gone downhill after we retired and moved back to southwestern Ontario in 2017. Not that it was cause and effect, just life and time and the way things turn out.

There'd been the Coronavirus Pandemic in 2020, followed by cycles of subsequent infections. Just when we thought we could cope with that ongoing reality, there'd been the Plague, the incursion of the mutated Ebola virus, starting in 2034. Worldwide economic collapse had followed. Added to that, an inexorably warming climate and worsening air quality that made it perilous to venture outdoors, some days.

And here I was in 2035, frowning out the window at the morning fog. Or was it smog? Maybe a little of both.

If only I could turn back time, I thought as I blended up my morning smoothie.

I can't, I thought. Then I paused. *But I can do something almost as good.*

$\infty \cdot \infty$

If I was hungry, I didn't know it, and a water bottle resting on the exercise bike's cup holder kept thirst at bay.

As I had on the previous days, I forced myself to do a half-hour workout. I'd been working through the *History of Dufferin County*, chapter by chapter. But my thoughts drifted as the narration droned in the background, and I kept checking the time remaining before I could go where I really wanted to. Back to our old property.

Once there, I did a long, slow lap of the outer trail, then stopped my bike at one particular spot that yielded a view of a long, sloping, tree-studded hill leading down into the county forest.

There I sat, the screen frozen with a view of the spot where we'd scattered Bandit's ashes after he succumbed to old age. I'd always thought this ridge would be a pleasant place to be laid to rest, with the rustling of poplar leaves, the fluting call of the wood thrush, the barred owl's *who-cooks-for-you* floating on the nighttime breeze.

The breeze.

I ran my hands along my arms. There *was* no breeze, though I heard a flicker's call through the speakers. The same flicker's call, repeated time after time, because I'd elected to stay in the same place.

I'm not here. Not really.

I gritted my teeth.

This is all an illusion, I told myself. *One I've entertained for long enough.* I tensed my leg muscles, preparing to push down on the pedals. To get moving out of here.

But what was the harm? More importantly, who really cared?

Nobody.

I settled back into position and stared at the screen, fighting a sense of defeat. I'd used the workouts to try to escape from my thoughts of the past. Ironically, I'd ended up mired in memory more deeply than before.

My sessions at the old place increased in duration day by day. By the end of the second week after I'd booked out the audio-vid, I took breaks only to eat, sleep, and tend to other daily needs.

Meanwhile, the grass grew longer outside, and the fridge grew emptier day by day.

~ • ~

After days of solitude, I heard something besides birdsong during my virtual visit of the old digs.

"There you are." A woman's voice.

Goosebumps formed on my forearms as I turned to look behind me. *How did somebody get in the house? I'm certain I locked all the doors.*

Nobody there. *Am I hearing things?*

Truly shaken, now—how far had I allowed myself to fall?—I looked at the screen, frowning.

And there sat Sheryl, on a silver mountain bike.

"How'd you get here?" I scowled at Sheryl's image on the screen.

She smiled, refusing to be put off. "The audio-vids were set up to be a group activity, if desired."

"Who said I wanted it?"

"Nobody." Her eyes narrowed. "But maybe you need it."

"What makes you think that?"

"Well, for one thing, you've let the audio-vid go overdue."

"Sorry." My upper lip curled.

"Secondly, your grass is getting long."

"Are you spying on me?"

"I drive past your place on the way to work."

"Fine. So I like to spend time here. Is that a crime?"

"Not one that will get you put in jail." She paused. "But you can't go on like this."

"What do you know about *this*?"

"More than you'd think." Sheryl sighed. "After Greer died, I went through something similar. Spending lots of virtual time in places we had fun. Too much time, to the detriment of other important things in my life."

"I'm sorry," I said. "I never asked about her."

"It's okay." Sheryl's smile looked strained. "This isn't real, you know."

"I know that. But it's real enough."

"The past is not a place where we can live. I learned that the hard way. Almost lost my job."

"I don't have a job to lose." True enough, though not exactly polite. I saw Sheryl recoil, stung by the sharpness with which I'd spoken.

If she leaves, I don't know if I'll have the courage to snap out of it.

After a brief internal struggle, I decided to admit aloud the thoughts that had preoccupied me the last few days. "With Allie gone, I'm not sure I know anymore how to live in the present. Sometimes I feel as though the best is behind me. That there's nothing to look forward to."

"You don't need to try to get through this alone."

I glanced around me. *Who else is here?* was my unspoken question.

If Sheryl noticed my gesture, she gave no indicator. "A group of us gets together every Tuesday to play virtual golf at the Sim-Dome. You'd recognize some of the women from the old days— softball, hockey. We've all lost our partners."

"Is that supposed to make me feel guilty? That I'm moping around as if I'm the only one it ever happened to?"

"You said that, not me."

I grimaced. "Allie was the social one."

"But you do like golf, right?"

"Haven't been since she—" I couldn't bring myself to finish the sentence.

"Next outing is Tuesday night at 7:00 p.m. You're welcome to come out." Sheryl offered a shy smile. "In fact, I hope you do."

She was holding out a life preserver, and I knew it. Part of me, perversely, wanted to rip it from her hands and throw it aside, to demonstrate the fact that I didn't need it, or her, or anything else. But another part recognized the gesture for what it was.

Genuine kindness. Caring, when I thought it didn't exist.

I've always had a stubborn streak. It's one of the things that made me a good athlete. The ability to keep plugging, to never give up, even when the scoreboard indicated the futility of that philosophy. "I don't need help," I said, pleased that the words came out without a quaver.

"If you say so." Sheryl shifted her weight and poised for departure. "Guess I'll have a look around while I'm here."

"Help yourself," I said, making a sweeping gesture to indicate the trail.

Sheryl rode away slowly. I watched her until she disappeared around a bend, then allowed the tension to ebb from my shoulders.

There. After a moment of weakness, I'd conquered the moment, as I had so many times in meetings, back in the day, when I'd maintained a veneer of composure in spite of a roil of feelings underneath.

But it didn't feel like victory.

Sheryl's departure left me feeling lonelier than before. Panicked, I looked in the direction Sheryl had ridden. I leaned my weight forward, ready to push off, then relaxed.

I had no idea how far she'd gone. Maybe she'd already left the simulation.

But I knew when, and where, I could find her.

Maybe I *could* get through this dark period of grief and loss by myself. But with a wisdom I'd lacked three weeks ago, I realized that to be wishful thinking. Denial of reality.

Perhaps it was time to abandon the old ways. To let emotion back in. To embrace friendship and allow myself to be vulnerable once again.

I lifted my head to look at the screen one more time. My finger hovered over the Stop button on the Dyna-Pedal. Resolutely, I pressed down. The scenery faded to black, and I blinked back tears. Only by sheerest resolution did I resist the temptation to fire the system back up and immerse myself once more in that place where I'd once been so happy.

But Sheryl was right. I couldn't stay here and survive. Not physically, and not emotionally.

I closed my eyes, and drew a deep, shuddering breath. My memories were all right here in my head, whenever I needed them.

Before I could change my mind, I walked over to the audio-vid player and ejected the disc. Maybe someday I'd check it out again for a ride down memory lane. Right now, I didn't trust myself to limit my time.

Besides, I had golf clubs to dust off. Maybe I could schedule a practice round before Tuesday.

I paused. *When is Tuesday, anyway?* In my funk, I'd lost track of the days.

I shrugged. I'd figure it out. With help if I needed it.

Grinning, I raced up the stairs. I stopped at the top and looked back down. Was I really ready to leave the past behind?

I thought of Allie, and drew in a sharp breath. I knew what she'd tell me if she were here to ask.

Get on with it.

I turned out the light and closed the door.

THE PRINCESS BOOK
❧ *Avery Vanderlyle* ❧

Kitty huffed as she pedaled furiously up the graded mountain road. The electric assist was doing all it could, but the route was steep and she wasn't used to this amount of exertion. Runs on the treadmill in her spaceship's exercise room didn't keep her as fit as she thought, apparently. Even for a small mountain.

She could have taken a jeep. It was right there; it would have been more convenient for her supplies, too. But the Portmaster of Fable's Shore had been sizing her up, and she'd passed others on the road out of town who'd looked at her appraisingly. One of her mission goals as an employee of the Cultural Authority was winning their trust, and that meant taking the bicycle and trailer.

This was her last stop on Sia V. In a couple of days she'd be traveling to the Interstellar Council's biennial meeting on Anov III where she was assisting the Archivists with their VR capture of the events. Fable's Shore wasn't the largest town, but the nearby mountains were a source of valuable minerals, and its port served native cities as well as other planets. She'd already assisted each household and institution in the town whose books needed repair or upgrading. She'd saved this trip—up the mountain to the prestigious Diamond View Academy—for the end.

Finally, the grade evened out, and she caught her breath. She could see the school's campus ahead of her: stone walls speckled with purplish moss and the angles of slate roofs beyond that. The school had a library, with books that needed repair and no appropriate way to bring the most delicate ones down to the spaceport. So she'd come to them.

She switched off the assist and let herself enjoy the last few minutes of her ride. The bike was old but sleek and finely tuned. Even the scattered dents added character, telling stories of long rides beneath the double suns, slippery winter paths, and dares along narrow tracks. Despite the trailer, the riding was easy. Kitty didn't spend much time outside. She'd missed the feel of fresh air rushing past her and the snatches of insect rumbling and bird whistling that she caught as she rode.

The gate to the school was open, and she rolled right into a huge courtyard. The short turquoise grass that passed for a lawn here added a bit of a bounce as she headed for the lone figure standing by the largest of the squat stone buildings.

The woman who stood waiting for her looked like a figure out of a book herself. She wore long gray robes flecked with silver. A black scarf covered her hair and wrapped around her face. A pair of flint gray eyes, bright against ochre skin, and a hint of a long straight nose peeked from under the cloth.

She bowed as Kitty approached. "Welcome, Bookbinder. I'm Dean Prima. We don't get many guests, but your arrival is especially fortuitous." She took a few steps forward, bending toward Kitty to whisper. "We need your help with the princess."

✧ • ✦

The book sat on a table in the library. *The Book of Blue Snow* was a popular folk history of Sia V's settlement, full of colorful figures and larger-than-life adventures printed on glossy pages as long as her arm. The full-color illustrations had been supplemented with glowing undertones and blinking lights. Several pages had augmented reality interfaces, others had barcodes that could be scanned to call up additional computer references.

Kitty pulled on her gloves and touched the page in front of her with awe. Books were living things to her, and volumes that had been upgraded and modified to reflect new technologies and customs never ceased to give her a thrill. She enjoyed old-fashioned preservation work, too, for families or institutions that wanted to keep a volume as close to the original state as possible. But renovating—adding digital components while maintaining the underlying essence of the book as a physical object—that was her highest calling.

The open pages displayed a full-color painting of a jungle with aquamarine vines twining up indigo trunks. Snakes hunted blue-and-gold-striped insects while brindled dogs nosed at rodents' burrows in the undergrowth. Leaves a dozen shades of blue and light green shadowed the area underneath and glowed where the sun's light hit them. Kitty stroked the margin with awe.

She pulled a pair of glasses from her bag and tapped the icon that opened her AR program. The jungle sprang to life: snakes slithered out of the foliage toward her, and a tiny blue-green shrew scampered into its den. An insect leapt toward her and she ducked, laughing.

The Librarian chuckled. "I commissioned that programming and it still surprises me." They were a scrawny figure whose robes were paler gray than the Dean's. Their matching scarf wrapped more loosely around their head, framing a face rich with laugh lines.

Kitty turned off the glasses and examined the pages once more, slowly flipping through them. "The princess's personality schema is really encoded here?"

The Librarian grinned proudly. "Encoded in several layers in the book for redundancy and security." They pointed to tiny, glittering embellishments along the edges of the book. "This is only one instance."

"She volunteered to undertake this hazardous procedure," the Dean replied. "It is her best chance to avoid the Draosian blockade and take our case to the Council."

The Dean had explained the situation to Kitty on the way to the library. The nearby Draosian culture was expanding, taking over other planets by force or by stealth. A few months earlier, they'd initiated a blockade of Sia that was strangling the planet's economy. Princess Viola had worked with the technicians and staff at the Academy to come up with a secret way to get herself off the planet.

"I understand now." Kitty said slowly. "You want me to take this book to the Council meeting." She rose to face them. "I—I'm part of the Cultural Authority. We can't get involved in politics."

The Dean bowed her head. "The blockade is illegal. The Council issued a statement denouncing it. But we are a poor, backwater system, not worth spending resources on. Princess Viola is a member of the sub-Council for this sector and has a right to petition the full Council to take action." She looked up to stare into Kitty's eyes. "You may call it interference to transport her through an illegal blockade to a conference where she has been invited. I don't." She spread her hands wide. "We don't have warships that can break the blockade. There are mercenaries who have offered to help . . . being in their debt would be as bad as submitting to the Draosians. Parliament is seriously considering the mercenaries, though."

"There would be bloodshed either way," the Librarian added. "But if the princess can get the Council to sanction the Draosians, then hopefully there will be no violence. Isn't violence an enemy of culture?"

Kitty traced the length of a vine on the page thoughtfully. "The saying goes, 'Violence is the antithesis of Cultural Cultivation.'" She looked at the gorgeous book with its hidden information. Kitty had watched some video clips of Viola and her mother, Queen Lilla. The monarchy's authority was limited to domestic ceremonial and cultural events, but they also played a part in interstellar diplomacy. Viola was a couple of years out of university, with a cheerful enthusiasm for her role in her public appearances. Undergoing this procedure to advocate for her people was another level of dedication.

The bookbinder's fingers skimmed the edges of a page where the gold was uneven. This was probably an artifact of the personality encoding, but it made Kitty think of a small scar on Viola's forehead from a childhood cycling accident. The princess could have had the scar removed, but kept it. Was the scar a reminder to keep going, a reminder it's important to take risks?

Kitty didn't like taking risks. But what would she see when she looked at herself if she didn't interrogate her ethics when the situation was complicated?

"I'll ask my pilot to do some research on the situation."

The Dean nodded. "The Cultural Authority encryption schemes should be safe."

"They're reset weekly by the Interstellar Council's Security AI. The Draosians wouldn't bother to try and break them." T'hrav would be more objective than she would be, with the Princess Book in front of her. But Kitty knew she couldn't walk away without that special volume under her arm.

She gestured to the other table where a pile of books waited. "Show me what you need with these. It's more important than ever that I do my job as usual."

~ · ~

The ride down was breathtaking. Kitty pumped the brakes more than once; the last thing she wanted was to hit a bump and lose control of the bike or trailer. The wind rushed past her, smelling of marshmallow and jasmine from spiky lavender blooms. Dragonflies as big as her hand darted past, wings shimmering. She thought of the scintillating encoding of the princess in her book, and smiled.

Portmaster Liam grinned back at her when she arrived, flushed and exhilarated.

"I knew you were the kind to ride," he said. "It's the only way to really know a place."

The Portmaster wore close-fitting black trousers and a beige sweater, accenting his copper skin. He had no scarf; he wasn't part of the Sian intellectual class who veiled their body in order to focus on the mind.

"I hadn't ridden a bicycle since I left university." She patted the bicycle and felt a pang of regret. "I'm grateful for the assist, though. I'm not as fit as I thought."

"It must be hard to get enough activity cooped up on that ship of yours." Liam looked thoughtful. "I have an old exercise bicycle in the shed. It needs a bit of work, but I'll trade it to you. Do you have any recent VRaction modules? They're slow to make their way out here."

Technically, VR modules were released by sector, Kitty knew, and isolated areas weren't always included. Savvy consumers had multi-sector adaptors on their systems, and Kitty had always considered those restrictions bureaucratic technicalities.

Plus an exercise bike was an interesting idea.

"I finished *Dogs of War III* last week," she said. "The gameplay was a bit derivative, to be honest, but the effects keep getting better."

Liam chuckled. "I don't care if it's derivative. It would be months before I got my hands on a copy. You have a deal." He whistled, and a cargo robot trundled over. He gave it instructions, and it rolled into a small metal building next to the main port tower. Moments later, the machine emerged carrying a slightly rusted, once-black stationary bike. Liam pointed it to the cargo hatch of Kitty's ship and it rolled off.

Liam helped her transfer her cargo onto the ship. There were a couple of other robotic haulers but no other humans around. Kitty saw a couple of shuttles that couldn't leave the atmosphere, but no other vessels capable of interstellar trips.

"It's very quiet," she commented, carrying a climate-controlled carrier that held a 2,000-year-old book she'd been commissioned to restore. One of Sia's original settlers had brought it to the newly terraformed planet, and she wasn't trusting robots with it.

Liam leaned in to answer, his voice barely more than a whisper. "The Draosian blockade has nearly destroyed our interplanetary commerce. Even our allies in the sector don't want to risk having a ship seized or damaged." His brown eyes narrowed. "We're hoping the Council will act. They said the blockade was illegal, but haven't done anything."

Did he know about Princess Viola's plans? Kitty patted the bag slung across her torso that held the Princess Book and decided not to bring it up.

"I'm sorry this is happening." Kitty answered. "Maybe something will be decided at the Council meeting."

Liam shrugged, frowning. "Proclamations won't stop the Draosians. Someone will have to act."

Kitty nodded. "I hope someone does."

She thanked him for his help and stepped into the ship, shooing the robots ahead of her into her workroom.

Kitty's pilot and only shipmate looked up from a book when Kitty strode into the kitchenette. T'hrav was a Formicitite, one of an insectoid race who lived communally. Once in a while, a Formicitite would leave their hive on a planet that also had human settlements and choose to join a human community. Most stayed on their home planet, but those who hungered to wander further learned skills that took them to the stars.

"I'm glad you made it back safely," she said. "I found some videos of that contraption you were forced to drive. It is terrifying, yes?"

Kitty laughed. "It's a rite of passage of sorts. It was a first sign to the Dean that I could be trusted."

T'hrav's antennae twitched "Did they have any choice?"

Kitty sighed. "They could have asked me to transport the book to their agent on Anov and not told me the princess is encoded in it. That might even have been the prudent thing to do."

"But the Draosians might try to stop us, yes, and that ignorance would be dangerous."

"It could be dangerous either way," Kitty said. "But I hope the weight of the Cultural Authority will keep things calm."

The alien rose, graceful on her lowest pair of limbs. "I'm glad they were honest with you. It is a disgrace the Council has not intervened yet. The more I read about this blockade, the more outrageous it seems."

"Someone is making money from this conflict, I'd guess. Even the members of the Council aren't immune to that."

"It should be exposed, yes?"

"Princess Viola will work on that." Kitty caressed the Princess Book idly. "Our job is to get her there."

T'hrav took the book from Kitty with a gentle touch. "I'll put it on a shelf. Best you don't know where it is. . . ."

"Just in case. Yes." Kitty sighed. "I'll prepare us for take off."

"We are a Cultural Authority ship," Kitty informed the hailing Draosian ship. "You have no right to board us." Their trip up and out of Sia's orbit had gone smoothly, but they had another day's travel before reaching the wormhole network that enabled interstellar voyages.

"All ships exiting the system must be checked for contraband," the mechanical voice replied. "The Cultural Authority respects the local statutes."

"Last I checked, this blockade was deemed illegal by the Council."

"It is the local statute," the voice replied. "We can shoot off your engines and then board you."

Kitty sighed. "I'm going to log a protest with the Council. But in the meantime, you can come aboard." She cut the communication with a gesture.

T'hrav's antennae twitched. "I read the cultural brief, but what should I know about the Draosians?"

"They are of human origin. Very hierarchical. They won't give us their names if they don't feel we're worth it." Kitty focused on her pilot. "They are speciesist, so, given that you're from a species they deem less important, they may ignore you entirely."

Her antennae twitched again. "I'm happy to fade into the background. I try not to draw undue attention to myself."

Minutes later, half a dozen autonomous drones floated through the airlock, accompanied by two uniformed Draosians.

"I'm Bookbinder Kitty Lennox, and this is Pilot T'hrav NW15. We have no contraband on board."

The larger of the Draosians gave her a solemn nod. She had bronze spiral epaulets on her black uniform. A dark blue choker indicating her gender stood out against her light-brown skin and brought out green flecks in her brown eyes. "I'm Sub-Praetor Ikor. Thank you for submitting to a search." She waved the drones on, and they zipped ahead, whirring slightly.

Her companion scowled. He was darker skinned, with a shaved head, and wore a sleeker black uniform with no visible ranks. The black lattice tattoo on his right wrist indicated a male-identified asexual.

He got straight to business. "We received reports of you bringing items on board."

"Everything I brought on board was legitimate. As a Bookbinder, I may bring books aboard that need time-consuming restoration work." Kitty glared at him. "Since I'm required at the Council meeting, I took a few more since I didn't have enough time at the Academy. I'm also authorized to buy or barter for some volumes that have cultural value."

The mobile the Draosian woman held pinged, and she glanced at it.

"The drones report biological materials in the kitchen. And both biologicals and digitals in unfamiliar configurations in the large room to the right of the kitchen."

"We bought some food for the journey home," Kitty replied. "It's always nice to add local cuisine to the pre-mades. Adds variety."

Ikor nodded. "And the biologicals and digitals?"

"I assume that's in the workroom. Those are books."

The man's eyes narrowed. "Books?"

"I'll show you." Kitty sighed. "Is Draosa one of those cultures that doesn't have books anymore? It's never been on my itinerary."

She led them down the short corridor to the workroom. A set of shelves held books she'd collected, some destined for the Archives on Anov and others personal favorites. On the other wall a series of climate-controlled boxes held ancient books she was in the process of restoring. A cabinet held supplies ranging from glue to leather sheets to tiny circuits, electrodes, and lights.

The drones were bobbing above the large table in the middle, where Kitty's work to upgrade a book was in process.

"We digitized all information a century ago," Ikor replied as they surrounded the table. "What books are left are in museums."

"Some cultures make that choice." Kitty pulled on a pair of gloves, picked up a scalpel, and cut between the book's pages and the board. "On ancient Earth, there was a long history of writing on stone and scrolls of various materials. The earliest books were made of animal skin, then plant-fiber paper became the standard. Lots of data was digitized, of course, when that technology became available, and there have been many attempts through the centuries to replace the paper in books with other materials. Today's paper is produced by bacteria, not trees, but it still contains similar plant fibers. That's your main biological component."

She pulled the innards of the book open and showed the delicate electronics stored in the hollow of the spine.

"With miniaturization, and with the easy ability to tweak the components of the paper, a new era of books began. There are microscopic wires in the pages themselves, powered by this small component. The battery will last for years. Some books even have solar panels in the covers to keep them running for longer."

"What's the point of all this?" The man's scowl had never left his face.

Kitty pulled a book with a shiny green cover from the shelf, and set it down on a free spot on the table. "I'll show you." She couldn't stop the smile growing on her face. "You probably don't have the VRaction program on your mobiles. Here." She snagged a pair of attuned glasses and handed them to him. He took them, still frowning.

The book was an atlas of Tuatis, a mostly tropical planet famous as a vacation destination. Kitty opened it to a page showing a waterfall flowing through a city. "Put the glasses on and look at the book."

When the Draosian agent hesitated, Ikor nudged him. "They're simple VR glasses with some directed audio, Tan. Let her show you."

With a shrug, Tan set the glasses on his face. Kitty watched as he peered at the page. It was one of her favorites. The VR lifted the scene off the page. You were there, standing on a railing looking over the waterfall while vendors hawked sausages and beer, and passersby chatted and strode along the cobblestone pathway. The VRaction module was extensive, and the viewer could "walk" for half a mile along the riverside promenade, so long as they kept holding the book.

The Draosian agent wasn't similarly thrilled, but his scowl faded to the smallest of frowns as he took in the scene. Abruptly, he flipped to a different page. This one displayed an ancient temple; Kitty knew the VR included a tour of the chapels and tower.

He pulled the glasses off and looked at her intently. "I see the appeal."

"That's good to hear." She exchanged a look with T'hrav. "As you can imagine, those electronics are delicate. I repair them. I add more limited features like bar codes and lights to older books that people want to integrate with modern technology. And I also repair older books that people want to preserve."

"That's fascinating." Ikor strode along the shelves, her drones floating behind her like a whirring, buzzing flock of balloons. "This one looks new." She pulled a large, glittering book from the shelf, and Kitty's heart sank.

It was the Princess Book.

"Yes, I sometimes also purchase books to bring to the Archive." She'd practiced saying that hundreds of times until it wouldn't trigger any superficial lie detection the drones had. Colloquially, it was even true: many people referred to the entire city as the Archive for the institution that dominated its economic and cultural life.

"It's a beautiful volume," she went on, channeling her nerves into enthusiasm. "Look at the artwork! Look at the gilding on the edges and on the cover. It has augmented reality interfaces on many of the pages—not as immersive as VR, but it is the style on Sia and many other worlds. This is a new edition of a classic, and I felt a copy was relevant as a cultural artifact."

Ikor was leafing through it. The drones hovered at her shoulder as if reading along.

"None of this happened." It was her turn to frown.

"They're folk tales, not history." T'hrav interjected.

Both of the Draosians glared at her. In response, T'hrav hunched over, curling in on herself. Of course the Formicitite was nervous, too. Kitty squared her shoulders, preparing to take the brunt of the agents' attention again.

"My pilot is correct. Folk history is about the tales a culture tells about itself. There are some wonderful digital references about the folk history of Sia that analyze this very collection." She pulled up a link on her wrist mobile then sent it to a screen above the desk in the corner of the room. The display lit up with the section where she'd left off, describing how a devastating series of winter blizzards just a couple of years after human settlement had inspired a series of survival stories featuring folk heroes who could control the weather.

"But I'm sure you're not here for a sociology lesson." She forced a smile. "Because I studied folklore and I could easily talk about this book for an hour based on what I've read so far." The agents didn't recoil, but Kitty hoped the sudden stiffness in their posture meant she'd distracted them from the book. "Is there anything else you'd like to examine, Officers?"

Tan looked at Ikor, who shrugged. She swiped across the screen of her mobile. The drones beeped. She shrugged again.

"There's nothing out of order here, given her profession."

Tan turned his scowl on her. "These books are all you brought on board?"

"Right. Some books, some food—"

"There's the exercise bicycle you've barely used." T'hrav offered hesitantly. Kitty hoped the agents couldn't interpret T'hrav's mandible clicks, which weren't hesitant at all. Distracting them from the books was a good idea.

The Draosians stared at her. Kitty flushed. "Yes. I—I did get an exercise bicycle."

Ikor raised an eyebrow. "Why?"

"Cycling is a cultural norm on Sia." Her wince wasn't forced. "One I hadn't realized I was out of shape for."

Tan's scowl was back. "Show us."

Ikor dropped the book carelessly on the table as they walked out of the workroom. Kitty forced herself to stay nervous, not to let any relief show until the Draosians were off the ship.

T'hrav had put together the exercise bike and made room for it in the rec space at the back of the mess hall. It was old, but with some oil and a new coat of paint, it was perfectly functional. T'hrav had added a VRaction interface so the rider could experience a country lane or a path through a tropical forest.

Ikor and Tan circled the machine carefully. A couple of the drones dipped in and out, flashing brief spears of lasers across the bike and beeping in low tones. Ikor pressed something, and all of the drones converged, hovering and chittering as they analyzed the machine.

"Explain this." Tan glowered.

"You've never seen a bicycle before, have you?" Kitty sighed. "T'hrav can show you some videos of the mobile version. On Earth, they were an important early personal transport machine. This one's stationary, used for exercising the legs and cardiac system." She swung a leg over. The control panel lit up automatically; she adjusted the incline and started pedaling. One of the drones made a startled beep and moved away just before she kicked it. Another bolted into the space in the middle of the frame, rotating and further examining the bike's internals.

"Seems tedious," Ikor pronounced.

Kitty thought of the rush of wind through her hair as she'd pedaled down the mountain, the Princess Book stored safely in her bag. She turned on the VR module and set it to project so all of them could see the scene. It wasn't too different from the path down from the Academy. The plants were Earth-like greens rather than Sia's blues, but she could still imagine the sweetness of the fresh air.

The drones continued to circle, beeping and humming as they examined her and her cycle.

"I don't know what your regimens for physical activity are," she adjusted the bike and pedaled faster. "But it's just me and T'hrav on this ship, so I mostly exercise alone.The exertion counteracts some of the physical impacts of space travel and the mostly sedentary work I do."

T'hrav gestured toward the large video screen at the other end of the room, and a clip of people cycling along the beach near Fable's Shore appeared on the screen.

"Bicycles are very popular on Sia." T'hrav added. "They are used for visiting friends, picnics, some work commutes, and other transit activities that don't require a lot of cargo. Cycling is encouraged as part of Parliamentary initiatives to maintain sustainability and to promote outdoor activities."

"Yes, but why did you buy one?" Tan eyed her suspiciously.

Kitty's pace faltered. Why had she bought one? The VR scene shifted, and she was suddenly in a meadow. Butterflies flitted by and a bright yellow bird dashed overhead.

"Before visiting Sia, I'd forgotten how much I used to love bicycling. There's no enclosure; you can feel and smell the air. You can see and hear what's around you. Would I have noticed the Sian dragonflies in a mechanical vehicle, for example?" She smiled. "It's the only way to really know a place."

"If bookbinding grows stale, you can transition to bicycle salesperson," Ikor said, a hint of a smile on her lips. She looked at her mobile once again. With a quick flick of her fingers, the drones floated up to hover by the ceiling. "There's nothing here that's not expected." She looked at Tan.

"Are you sure?"

She checked her display again. "As sure as I can be without taking it apart. I checked some specs from the Council databases and everything is in alignment. I even found the original catalog specifications." Ikor considered. "Perhaps this was a decoy."

Tan pursed his lips, face stony. "There was that ship last week; I would have impounded it for further investigation but HQ let them go. We were probably fed bad information—would the Sians really get the Cultural Authority involved?"

Kitty gave him a glare. "You've already involved the Cultural Authority. But if you're done here, my delay will be minimal."

Tan waved a hand at her dismissively. "You'll make it to the Council meeting with time to spare, Bookbinder." He glanced at his watch and tapped it three times in quick succession. "There's nothing here, Ikor. Time to go."

Kitty breathed a sigh of relief as they exited the ship with their entourage of drones.

"That was cl—" She stopped when T'hrav shook her head and tapped her left antenna. The pilot was right. They'd have to check the ship for listening devices. "—clearly a waste of time."

"I wonder what they were looking for?" T'hrav replied with an exaggerated shrug.

"We'll probably never find out." Kitty didn't have to fake the frown on her face. "Please get us back up to speed and prepped for the wormhole jump. I need a long ride on the exercise bike. I have to burn off some excess energy before writing a complaint to the Council. I wouldn't want to accidentally start a war."

༄ • ༄

Viola met her halfway up the mountain. The princess's bicycle was purple with garish gold trim and tassels hanging off the handlebars. She'd pulled off her violet head scarf and knotted it around her neck, letting her black hair float in a nimbus around her head. The scar on her forehead was there. It wouldn't have been encoded with her personality and memories, so Viola must have asked for it to be recreated. Kitty was right; it must be important to the princess. Kitty wanted to ask about it, but she'd wait until she knew Viola better.

The princess tutted when she saw the heavy trailer Kitty was towing.

"We can't race when you're hauling that."

"R-race?" Kitty felt her cheeks flushing. She'd used the exercise bike every day on the way to the Council meeting and back to Sia, but she wasn't in shape for a race up a mountain.

Viola laughed. "We used to do it when I was in school. We'd take a day trip to Fable's Shore, then turn off the assist and race on the way up."

"Why not race down?"

The princess grinned widely. "We raced down, too, but it's more dangerous that way. We weren't stupid. And going up is harder. . . ."

Kitty could vouch for that.

She'd last seen Viola in a stylish russet suit, her hair in complex braids beneath her scarf, as she eloquently described the dangers of the Draosian expansionist advances that included the takeover of two planets' governments as well as the blockade of Sia.

The Sian Princess had spent the Council time in a whirlwind of diplomacy and networking. Despite her urgency, and a lingering headache from being reconstituted out of the book encoding, she'd had time to thank Kitty. She made sure Kitty knew she and T'hrav would be honored guests on Sia at any time.

Viola's negotiations were successful. The Council had ordered two Enforcer warships to disrupt the blockade while they investigated. Kitty hoped this was more than a temporary solution. Viola had been pleased, though, and insisted Kitty get a round of applause from the Sian Parliament during a VR call with them.

"The Prime Minister would like to meet you," Viola said, as if following Kitty's thoughts.

Kitty had to get over this blushing habit. "I've heard there are some fabulous books in the Parliamentary Library."

"I'm sure there are." The princess cocked her head, looking at Kitty thoughtfully. "I know you don't want to publicize what you did, but surely we can find a way to honor you and your pilot."

Kitty looked up the slope. In a few minutes, the Academy would come into view. She looked forward to showing the book updates and repairs she'd made to Dean Prima and the Librarian. They'd promised her a hearty dinner and a performance by the Academy Choir. She'd have the chance to talk more with Viola, who grew more charming by the minute.

"I don't need any honors." She smiled. "T'hrav asked if I could pick up some Sian honeycomb for her." The pilot was attending a conference and would be back in five days. Kitty was looking forward to spending her free time on Sia.

"The honeycomb will be arranged tonight." The Sian snorted. "That's easy."

It was so nice cycling with Viola next to her. The path was still steep, but much easier than it had been the last time. All that exercise was paying off. There were still dragonflies and shiny blue beetles that zigged and zagged comically in the air trying to avoid them. Something different was in bloom, adding a cinnamony tang to the air.

The princess sneezed. "The Sweetbark pollen gets to me." She gave Kitty a mock glare. "As the heir to the constitutional monarchy of Sia, I command you to think of a way we should honor you." She grinned. "Before my mother fobs some old jewelry off on you."

"Maybe I like jewelry."

Viola looked her up and down. Kitty's usual uniform of a dark blue jacket, white shirt, and black trousers was unadorned except for her wrist mobile and an embossed bracelet of black cork.

"You don't like jewelry."

Kitty giggled. "I don't like jewelry. And I couldn't accept a gift like that."

"You see." The princess pouted. "Come up with something else."

The grade leveled off. Soon they'd be at the Academy. Kitty turned off the assist and pedaled a little faster. Just because.

Viola laughed and sped up to match her. A dragonfly the same color as the princess's bicycle dashed between them and darted off toward the school. Kitty imagined speeding along with her new friend, laughing together. Breathing the scented air, trying to catch the dragonflies. Testing her endurance.

"I thought of something. There's an original copy of *The Book of Blue Snow* in the Royal Country House. My predecessor helped restore it. The Country House is pretty remote, though."

"The gardens there are gorgeous," Viola grinned. " I can take you there—it's not unusual that a representative of the Cultural Authority would want to visit." She straightened. "It's decided. We'll spend a couple of days. I'll take you around the countryside; there are some lovely cycling routes." She paused to look into Kitty's eyes. "I'll show you everything."

Was Kitty's heart beating faster at the thought, or was it the cycling? Her fingers gripped tightly around the handlebars, and she matched the princess's grin. "Can we fit in a race or two?"

Delight lit up Viola's face. "I'm counting on it."

THE WHEELS OF FALSE GODS
✢ Taru Luojola ✢

*T*n the beginning, the gods created earth for themselves to live on. When the earth was ready, they found it good, and they dug their roots deep into the fertile soil. They created humans and raised and nurtured them so that humans could serve the gods.

The gods told the humans: "Our flesh shall be your food and our blood shall be your drink, and you are what you consume. Out of us you build your houses and weave your clothes. There's enough of us for everyone, as that is how it's meant. In your speech you will utter our names, you will honor us in everything you do, as without us you poor things wouldn't even exist." And humans cared for and worked this warm soil where the rivers run from mountains to the sea and the gods prosper and allow humans to flourish.

But one day, the stones whispered unto humans: "You don't need gods for everything. They are your food and drink, but we can offer you much bigger houses, much greater cities, and much stronger weapons. Serve us and subordinate your old gods as your servants." And humans chipped false idols on stone and subordinated their old gods as their servants. They built big houses, great cities, and strong weapons. They divided themselves into those who have and those who don't and forgot to serve their gods.

Then the gods' wrath came upon humans, and the gods stopped bearing fruit, and humans didn't have anything to eat and drks—

Seedbraider Arara froze with terror. They stared at the seed braid which they had been running between their thumb and forefinger. Could it really be so that the holy braid had been braided incorrectly? No, the seeds had been damaged, so that *i* looked like *k* and *n* looked like *s*. And not only these two seeds, but a long section of the braid was moist and spoiled.

"Oh holy papaw!" Arara exclaimed.

Other braiders turned to look. Arara raised the braid so that everyone could see it.

"We have to go through all the braids before they're destroyed," they said to the braiders.

"Destroyed?" Tapi-ira was shocked to say. "All of them?"

"There are hundreds of them!" Iagura said.

"What's destroying them?" Tapi-ira asked.

"Water," Arara said. They looked up and saw wet spots in the wooden ceiling of the braidery. "The rains have even destroyed our roof!"

Other braiders started to mutter in panic and closely examine the braids in their hands. They cried out when they found mold, sprouting, or deterioration.

"In the name of the holy ananas, why do gods try us so?" Iagura wailed.

"We must make copies of them all, and quick," Arara said.

"The roof must be repaired before that, otherwise we'll be working in vain," Tapi-ira said.

"And we don't have enough seeds," Iagura said.

Arara swallowed. Iagura was right. The rainy season had been heavy. It had destroyed other houses, too, and washed roads away, but the worst thing was that even the trees and fields had suffered, and the harvest was bad. They'd have seeds to copy only a fraction of the braidery's collection, and in this situation every new braid was away from future harvests. The gods were really trying them.

Iagura cleared their throat. "If only neither fire nor water could destroy the holy scriptures. . . ."

They left the thought hanging in the air. The braiders were side-eyeing each other.

"Do you want even more of the gods' wrath upon us?" Tapi-ira at last burst out. "Tore'a chipped a picture of an ananas on stone and got their punishment. If you take that path, it will await you too."

Iagura didn't reply. They all had a bit too lively memories of how Tore'a, doused in ananas juice, was screaming when ants and wasps ate them alive. And after that came the heavy rains. One mistake, and the furious and hungry people would storm the braidery again and tear the place down.

"We don't carve any holy scriptures on stone. We will only braid seeds, as always. We'll start with copying the most important ones," Arara said. They were a leader now, after all, when Tore'a was no more. "First the holiest braids. And the rest . . ."

They couldn't talk about how the braids would be destroyed. Saying it would make it too real.

"There are copies of the holiest braids in other cities. We can get those later. Let's instead make copies of those rare braids that we have only here," Tapi-ira suggested. "And then let us pray that the next harvest will be ready before the rest of the braids are destroyed."

"The next harvest won't grow so fast," Iagura said and shook their head.

"But the gods—"

"The gods want to see how we find a way out of this trial," Tapi-ira interrupted Arara.

"Why don't we send a runner to bring us enough seeds to copy all the braids?" Iagura asked to restore harmony.

Arara saw how Tapi-ira wavered. "Yes, that's what we do," Arara said quickly.

"Can we get the seeds in time? A week to the capital, another back here," Tapi-ira said.

Iagura lowered their eyes. "Yes. That's long enough for the braids to become illegible."

"Well, let's give some of the braids to the runner to take them to the capital for copying. We'll get them back later. Meanwhile, we could use the little seeds we have left to make copies of the most damaged ones here," Arara announced their decision.

☞ • ☜

Ka-aapivara stood in attention and listened to the instructions of the seedbraiders.

"These braids you'll leave in the capital for copying," Arara said and handed over a big scroll of cloth. "And this is a list of seeds that you must bring here as fast as possible."

Ka-aapivara slipped the scroll over their back and took the braided list. They scanned it through. "These seeds will weigh as much as dozens of ananases. I'm not sure if I can carry a load this big. Not even if I used wheels."

"In that case—" Arara began, but Tapi-ira interrupted them.

"Are you talking about silver wheels?"

Ka-aapivara swallowed and nodded.

"How dare you mention silver in here?" Tapi-ira bellowed.

"They seem to live well enough in the Sunset Mountains, even though they make lots of things out of silver," Ka-aapivara found courage to say. They had seen the shiny houses when they had ran there to exchange fruit for wheels. "I haven't seen the gods punishing—"

"The Sunset People live among stones and have fallen for stones. They don't have trees—the gods have abandoned them already. They would starve without our fruit. The stones don't have power over here. Don't challenge the gods," Tapi-ira preached.

"Tapi-ira, we don't have time to wait. The gods want to see how we find a way out of this trial," Arara said. They turned to Ka-aapivara. "As the high braider, I say: take the wheels."

Ka-aapivara was quick to nod. It was dangerous to witness how the braiders argued with each other. Ka-aapivara was just anxious to get on the move.

Arara held out another braid. "If need be, take another runner from the capital to help you. We must get the seeds. Here's an authorization with our seals."

Ka-aapivara took the authorization. Every braider had braided their own seal in it. With this authorization Ka-aapivara could get anything from the capital. On their way there, nobody would deny them a bed, and they'd get as much to eat and drink as they needed.

"And take care that the braids don't get any more moisture during your travel. I'm afraid that should that happen, they won't be legible when you get there," Arara finished their briefing.

Ka-aapivara made a formal greeting by raising their fingers to their forehead as a symbol for ananas leaves and exited the braidery. Without wasting time, they hurried to the runners' headquarters, showed their authorization, and took wheels. There was only one of them in the city, and this surely was an emergency. They pushed the wheels in the narrow streets where it was hard to ride. The atmosphere on the street was appalling. Those who were able were shoveling mud out of their houses and trying to repair the streets and patch leaking roofs with logs that were already swollen and turf that was soaked. Those who were too hungry were laying in the shade and could do nothing but wait for better times. The sentence *trust the gods and you will be fed* was spelled out by the arrangement of the trees lining the street, in stark contrast to what Ka-aapivara could see.

Ka-aapivara arrived to a buzzing square. Hungry people alarmed by the bad harvest were crowding around the stalls and pleading for fruit, vegetables, and meat, as storekeepers tried to create some order by shouting. Ka-aapivara was efficient with their elbows, which gained them many angry words.

"Give way, I have an authorization from the braidery!" they cried and waved the authorization.

"The braidery should go to the field and do something useful," someone snapped.

"Come here, come here!" a storekeeper shouted and beckoned to Ka-aapivara.

"Don't skimp on the rations, I have to hurry to the capital," Ka-aapivara said and handed over their bag to the storekeeper.

"Do you think you're more important than us?" a crooked and wrinkled old person demanded.

"I'm on a gods' mission," Ka-aapivara answered. The mob roiled and pushed them from all sides. "Be careful now, my people! This scroll is full of holy braids!"

"A gods' mission, you say! Tell those gods to give us a proper harvest," the old person grumbled.

"Watch your words," someone interjected, and the old person got into a nasty argument with some gods-abiding person. Ka-aapivara didn't want to get dragged into it, so they turned back to the stall. There were scruffy-looking fruits on the back shelf, arranged to spell out the words: *without us you wouldn't exist.*

What's wrong with the gods? Ka-aapivara wondered.

The storekeeper interrupted Ka-aapivara's pondering by handing the bag back to them. "Do you need anything else?"

"Chilled maté, please. Fill 'em all up," Ka-aapivara asked and gave them ten huge calabashes.

The storekeeper raised their brows. "You're emptying the whole stall!"

"Just fill 'em up, please. I have to get over the mountains, and the sooner I'm there, the quicker the gods are to be appeased. I don't have time to stop and brew any drinks."

The storekeeper grunted and shook their head but went to fill the calabashes up anyway.

After getting their rations, Ka-aapivara packed them in the bags attached to their wheels and hit the road. They let the invaluable scroll of braids stay on their back, as it didn't weigh much and the rains were over, anyway. The words of gods on the trees along the main road wished them to travel obediently.

The wheels were made of hardwood and silver because the gods hadn't given them any other material dug out of stone. By sitting on the wheels and kicking the ground, it was possible to get to the capital in just three days, much faster than by walking. The saddle was made of jaguar hide and was comfy to sit on, and the wheel spokes ended in soft leathery toes that pounded on the muddy road under Ka-aapivara one after another. It was easy to travel when it didn't rain, and in no time, Ka-aapivara had crossed the plateau.

Before climbing the mountain, Ka-aapivara stopped to eat. The sun was edging closer to the horizon, but the first mountain way station was still far away. One really had to hurry when the journey didn't start first thing in the morning. They gobbled their food and started off to push the wheels uphill. When they were halfway up, it became dark. Ka-aapivara took a lantern, fired it up, and hung it in front of the wheels. They could see the road but not much else.

Finally, Ka-aapivara arrived at the way station. They were nearly exhausted when they walked their wheels into the cave. A guard stepped out to eye them.

"Good evening, Mobia," Ka-aapivara greeted the familiar face.

"Well, isn't it Ka-aapivara! Why are you running here in the night?" the guard asked.

"Braidery business," Ka-aapivara said and showed their authorization.

"Come over here then, I'll give you the best place to sleep. You're the only one sleeping here tonight," Mobia said. "Do you want to lay down right away, or would you come here by the fire first?"

"Thank you! I'm glad to chat for a while before I fall asleep," Ka-aapivara said and walked with their stiff legs to the fire. Only there they took the braid scroll off their back. It wasn't good to let it away from one's eyes even for a moment, even though there weren't any other people than Ka-aapivara and Mobia.

"So, what's your important business?" Mobia asked conversationally.

"I'm taking some braids of the gods to the capital," Ka-aapivara said and gnawed on dried grasseater meat.

"On braidery business and using silver wheels?" Mobia asked.

"This is an emergency. The braidery granted me their permission, they surely are in a hurry with these braids."

"What a time to be alive. I wouldn't have believed that the braidery would abandon their own teachings."

Ka-aapivara shrugged. "I guess these times are a bit odd, sure. But will the gods really get angry if we use silver? The people on the Sunset Mountains seem to live all right, even though they dig silver out of the ground."

"Well, it's not my job to think such things. Let the learned people interpret the gods, and I'll take care of my own stretch of this road," Mobia said. "Speaking of which, it's time for me to go on a patrol again. You can go to sleep, the patrol will take a while."

Ka-aapivara nodded and yawned. Mobia got up and walked out of the cave, and Ka-aapivara limbered up their tired arms. Oh how sweaty their shirt was, even though it hadn't been a hot day. Sweat literally still ran down their back.

And then a terrible thought hit Ka-aapivara's mind. They checked the braid scroll, and oh yes, it too was soaked in sweat. How could they have made such an elementary mistake? Hadn't the braider especially underlined that the scroll shouldn't get wet, and now Ka-aapivara, blinded by their important mission and their head higher than the hungry citizens', had forgotten the most important instruction!

Quickly, they opened the scroll and looked at the braids. The worst had indeed happened: some of the braids had been moistened, and here and there there were crumbled seeds. If they moved the scroll even a little bit, the crumbs would drop away and the words of gods would turn into dust on the cave floor. There was no way the braids would make it to the capital.

What to do? What to do?!

The fire threw dancing shadows on the cave wall. Ka-aapivara got a desperate idea. Yes, they had seen what had happened to that braider who had carved on stone. The whole city had seen. But that had been a time of plenty, and they had done their crime out of hubris, not desperation. Surely the gods would understand that this was an emergency?! Ka-aapivara touched the wall and found the stone was soft and porous. It could be possible to use a sharp bone knife to scratch the images of the gods and the words they made on the cave wall. There they'd wait until Ka-aapivara returned from the capital, and, when they got back here, they could stop to make rough braids from the words so the seedbraiders back home could use them to make their own beautiful copies.

"Oh gods, forgive me this terrible disgrace I'm about to commit, but know that I'm doing this for you," Ka-aapivara muttered and started to scratch the first picture of a fruit.

It was slow work. There were so many words, and every word had so many fruits, and in the flickering light it was hard to see what the crumbled seeds on the scroll cloth were. And when the first braid would be scratched, there would be a second one, and then a third one, then fourth and fifth, and it would in no way be possible to get the job done before dawn. Ka-aapivara cried and cussed, sweated and groaned and squinted over the braids with their tired eyes, and they kept scratching with their aching arms, because they had a duty to the words of gods.

Mobia was returning from their patrol when they spotted a jaguar in the darkness. Only the ear of a seasoned guard who had spent years in the mountains could have discerned the almost inaudible beast creeping closer. Mobia held a pike in one hand and a torch in the other and rushed towards the beast, crying hard as they ran. The jaguar flashed its teeth, but the torch waving here and there held it back.

"Run off now, you beast!" Mobia shouted and kept swinging the torch.

Little by little, the huge beast backed off. Mobia kept shouting and pushed the jaguar away from the cave. If you gave them even an inch, they'd keep coming to the cave. The next moment they'd be attacking travelers, and that's not what Mobia was going to allow on their stretch.

The jaguar accepted its defeat and vanished into the bushes. Mobia strained their ears and, after hearing nothing, returned to the cave. They swung the torch a few times more before stepping in so that the beast wouldn't get the idea of returning.

This night was safe. But the jaguar would be back tomorrow, and the night after that, and again and again until the gods were appeased. The nights were secured one at a time, and that was Mobia's job. They rested the pike on their shoulder and stepped into the cave.

"Another jaguar," they said to Ka-aapivara." I wonder why they've been running around here lately. As if gods wanted to pun—"

Mobia couldn't believe their eyes. Ka-aapivara had been carving idols on the wall. No wonder the gods wanted to punish!

"You, runner, stop that right now!" Mobia gave an order.

They rushed to Ka-aapivara and pulled them away from the wall. Ka-aapivara yelped and dropped on their buttocks, but Mobia had already forgotten them because they had a more important thing to do. They grabbed a loose stone and started to chip the idols off the wall.

"Don't destroy them!" Ka-aapivara cried and jumped on Mobia's neck.

Mobia tried to shake Ka-aapivara off their neck, but the runner kept on. Mobia tried to keep chipping the idols, but Ka-aapivara swayed so much that it wasn't easy.

"So, you want the gods to punish us?" Mobia bellowed. "Weren't the torrents enough, eh?!"

"The braids are broken! If you destroy the carvings, the words of the gods are lost!"

"You can't carve the words of gods in stone. Everyone knows that. Get off me and let me do my job," Mobia groaned and struggled to get Ka-aapivara off them.

"Never!" Ka-aapivara cried.

They lost their hold and dropped off Mobia's back, and the guard got back to chipping the wall. Desperate and tired, Ka-aapivara pounded Mobia's back with their fists with no effect. They jumped up and tried to hit Mobia's arm. The guard brushed Ka-aapivara away like a bug.

Ka-aapivara didn't give up, and soon Mobia felt their skin pricking, like the runner was hitting them with a knife. That made Mobia angry, and they turned around, alas, just at the same moment Ka-aapivara brought their hand and the knife down. The blade sunk into Mobia's neck, the guard yelped in surprise and lost their grip on the stone.

Ka-aapivara fumbled backwards. Mobia dropped on their knees and tried to grab the knife handle. How did this happen? Mobia opened their mouth, but no words came out. Terrified, Ka-aapivara took a step back, turned around, and ran away out into the night. Mobia was alone. They dropped onto all fours, and blood got mixed with sand. Their eyes blurring, they caught a glimpse of the braid scroll that Ka-aapivara had left there. Perhaps the words of the gods would give them some strength. They grabbed the scroll and pulled it closer. They felt stronger already. But not much. Mobia tugged the scroll under their arm and didn't see how crumbs of seeds dropped on the ground. With their last breath, they crawled into their den, laid down on their pallet and, nursing the words of the gods, fell asleep for the last time.

∽ • ∾

Arara squinted at the frail braid. It was hard to distinguish the rotten seeds from each other. *For . . . g . . . ing . . .* no, it couldn't be right . . . *for . . . e . . . ing . . .* It was slow and exhausting work, their hand picking up seeds from bowls that were getting emptier and emptier by the hour.

But the braiders had to make do with what they had. The citizens were on the verge of a mutiny after it was found out that idols were carved on the wall of the nearest mountain way station and the night guard was murdered. Everyone was looking for the missing runner, truncheons in their hands, although it was generally thought that jaguars had got them because no god would let such a deed go unpunished.

No other runner was willing to work for the braidery. "You have your holy protection, but nothing protects us from the furious people," the runners said. "We had to leave the wheels in the cave, who would fetch them for us? Please, tell the people that the braidery accepts the wheels."

The braidery couldn't do anything for the situation. The guards wouldn't go near the runners, and, for their own safety, the runners stayed away from the guards. Because of this, the runners couldn't run the road to the capital. It had already become impossible to save all the holy braids. And it was better to not mention the cave, so that people wouldn't come to blame the braiders for the carved idols.

There was some noise of a running mob outside, and it got closer. Arara froze and eyed Tapi-ira and Iagura. Without uttering a word, they reached an understanding. If the mob rushed in, their time as braiders of the gods would be over, that's how little they were listened to and respected any more. The best they could do would be to try to get people to leave the braids alone and not destroy them and burn the braidery down. It was shocking to accept that they had to take this kind of possibility into account.

The noise grew louder, and Arara could discern footsteps and individual voices. But the mob ran past the braidery. People were shouting about the river and something about a big boat. The defeated faces of the three braiders turned to look surprised.

"Should we go and have a look?" Tapi-ira asked.

"Of course. We are still braiders, after all," Arara said.

They put their gorgeous leaf hats on their heads and walked as a group to the river. There really was a big boat sailing up. If you could call something that huge a boat. Even the biggest palace was nothing compared to it. On the top flew a flag whose foreign colors glowed in the afternoon sun.

"Are the gods coming to us?" someone asked excitedly.

"There's surely food on that boat," storage keepers cried. "Go and get some baskets ready!"

"We're saved!" many people were shouting.

But Arara couldn't feel joy. The boat looked ominous. The bow carried a strange and false idol. The pipes sticking out of its sides were not wooden. They were some kind of stone that looked even more sinister than the silver from the Sunset Mountains.

People noticed that the braiders had arrived. A storage keeper asked: "So, are the gods finally appeased?"

Curious faces turned to look at Arara. Their pulse raced. They raised their hands to calm people down. And then they noticed that they still held in their hand the half-rotten braid they had been copying. Their eyes locked on the braid, and the world around ceased to exist. If they had still seen what the people were doing, Arara would have noticed that everyone had turned to look at the braid as if it contained the answer to the keeper's question.

And perhaps it did.

. . . *And then foreign people from a faraway land arrived who bowed to false gods of stone. "Haven't we suffered enough?" the people pleaded to the gods. But the gods were not appeased, and they watched silently as the aliens subordinated the people with their stone and silver. Curse after curse fell upon people, and the people prayed for the gods to have mercy.*

At last the gods spoke upon them: "It is too late for you to repent. Warning after warning was sent to you, but you kept bowing to your stone idols. Can you eat stone? Can you drink silver? Now join those who are perished by stone, you ungrateful people."

TRUE STORIES OF CYCLING ON CERES

❧ Christopher R. Muscato ❧

"**I** never understood why anybody would do that," Lutetia frowns out the window.

"Don't ask me to explain it." Hektor shrugs, then nods politely at the passing cyclist. She returns a slight wave, legs pumping and wheels spinning as she shrinks into the distance behind them.

"It doesn't even seem safe."

"We're here," Hektor announces, the cyclist no longer within the range of his attention span. Instead, his boyishly twinkling eyes are fixated on the destination ahead. Lutetia can't help but crack a small smile as she observes him, and tries to remind herself why this trip matters. He's talked about coming back here for years, recreating the trail he took with his father, camping as they had done. Lutetia twists herself enough to peer into the seat behind her.

"Iris," she coos, and the bundle of safety harnesses stirs. "Wake up, sweetie."

As Hektor engages the gravity lock and the wings vibrate, Lutetia glances one last time outside the window. Maybe it's just her imagination, but she thinks she can make out the outline of the cyclist, still pedaling through the black, a miniscule speck dwarfed by the gargantuan disk of swirling red and orange hues rising behind her. The travel brochures all claimed the view of Jupiter was great from here. At least that was true.

❧ • ❧

"Vesta family, here's your reservation. First time visiting the Asteroid Belt?" The camp manager asks, handing over a set of keys. Hektor snatches them with haste.

"My father used to bring me when I was a kid," he explains, glee in his voice. "Now I get to bring my daughter."

"Should be a bit nicer than you remember," the manager rolls a toothpick between his lips and jerks his head towards the window. "Lot of updates been made ever since the Belt exploded as a tourist destination. There was a time it was only the pretty serious deep-space campers who stopped through here."

"That was my dad," Hektor puffs his chest and smiles, radiating warmth and affection. Lutetia squeezes his hand. She knows the loss still hurts.

The camp manager uploads a map onto their tablet and points out their campsite. There are air-locked tunnels connecting each hab with the larger facilities, he says, but they'll want to park their ship by their hab so they should keep those space suits on for now. Hektor and Lutetia load Iris back into the ship, secure her safety harnesses, zip over to the campground, readjust her helmet in case she managed to loosen it, wrestle the squirming child from her seat, and start dragging bags from the ship to the hab. Even small tasks require a substantial investment of time and energy with a toddler, but it will be worth it to see her face from atop Ahuna Mons, basking in the glow of a million stars. At least, that's the image that Hektor and Lutetia have seared into their expectations. Hektor sees himself as he remembers his father, an anchor, little Iris clutching his strong hand as she marvels at the immensity of the Universe. Lutetia can already imagine the holo-frame she wants to hang in the family room of Iris under the stars. The hike should at least make for some great pictures.

Their hab is a small dome, just big enough to stand up and walk a few paces. Cozy, Hektor calls it. Lutetia prefers the word cramped, but then she never had Hektor's fondness for squeezing into tight quarters just to "reconnect" with the pristine natural wonders of space, nor his nostalgia for deep-space camping. She sighs to herself as she sets up the cots. It makes him happy, and it's a good experience for Iris.

That evening, the family takes dinner in the mess hall, a larger dome with magnificent windows through which to view the sparkling diamonds of distant stars and the looming shadows of passing asteroids shuffling as their orbits adjust to changes in Jupiter's gravitational pull.

"Whassat?" Iris taps a small finger on the window. Lutetia bends down next to her and sees a small vessel approaching the landing site.

"It's called a solar-cycle," Lutetia explains, one eyebrow involuntarily arching as she recognizes the tiny craft they had passed on their flight in. "People use them to get around, but they're much slower than our ship. Come on moonbeam, let's go get dessert."

"Thycle," Iris tries the word, feeling it on her tongue as she bounces along at her mother's side. Lutetia can't help but glance back out the window to see the solar-cycle dock, a woman dismount. A few minutes later, as Lutetia is helping Iris spoon a mound of Kuiper cobbler into her mouth, the airlock opens and the woman strides in, shaking her short hair loose of the helmet. She is quickly greeted by a few others, hugs are exchanged, and she disappears into the crowd. Lutetia watches all of this from the corner of her eyes. She had noticed some solar-cycles already parked outside when they arrived. Must be a few of the weirdos camping here this week.

∾ • ∾

Lutetia sees the cyclist several more times. Whenever her family visits the mess hall, the cyclist is there. Sometimes she's working on pieces of her solar-cycle, tinkering with gears or the housing for the electromagnetic conductors that spin as she pedals, but most of the time she's talking with other cyclists. No, not talking, not really. The other cyclists are doing the talking. This woman looks like she's just listening.

Lutetia doesn't know why the cyclists are so often on her mind. They have solar-cyclists in their neck of the solar system too; it's not the most common sight but not that unusual either.

She tries to put the thought away as they prepare for their hike up Ahuna Mons. Hektor fiddles with their hiking suits, adjusting the air capacity and calibrating the grav boots to Ceres's gravity. He swears he knows what he's doing. Lutetia tries not to notice all the cussing escaping his lips, agitated grumbles filling their small living space as he sets up the gear. She plays with Iris, zipping a plush spaceship around the child's giggling head. Hektor talks about doing this with his father as a boy, but he's certainly never done any deep-space hiking since they met, and that was twelve years ago. Maybe she'll have the camp manager check their suits just to be safe.

After a few small hikes to acclimate their bodies and break in the never-before-worn hiking regalia, the day arrives. Up early, Hektor and Lutetia help fit each other into the lean hiking suits, securing extra oxygen tanks to Hektor's back just in case the O_2 reclaimers in the suits fail; an unlikely scenario, but still, it never hurts to take precautions. Iris is eventually coerced into her miniature suit, wriggling and screaming until she stands before them like an irritated snowman, too poofy and bulbous to merit much range of movement. Hektor secures Iris onto Lutetia's back; the lower gravity here has its advantages when carrying a toddler up a mountain.

The trail itself is well marked, Ahuna Mons being the most popular destination on the Asteroid Belt's most traveler-friendly asteroid. They slip and slide a little on the icy sediment, but the boots help to steady their steps. At least the other hikers seem to be faring about as well.

Finally, the trio reach the top. Lutetia reaches out and grasps Hektor's hand. Below them, Ceres's twinkling gray surface rounds in a vista of small craters and ridges, shadow and light dancing across the surface, reflecting the movements of countless celestial bodies through the heavens above. And as for the heavens, Lutetia has to admit: Hektor was right. It's not the same as seeing it from the ship's window.

Hektor helps ease Iris off Lutetia's back, and the toddler sprints across the open space, thrilled at having such unrestricted movement in the minimal gravity, bouncing as much as running in the puffy suit. Hektor chases after her, laughing and shouting in joy, and Lutetia hangs back to watch. It's rare to have a moment come to fruition so beautifully. She wants to enjoy it for a minute. Then she'll take a few pictures.

Lutetia is just firing up the holo-lens in her helmet when a flash of metal crests the mountain's summit, traversing the trail designated for solar-cyclists. The tiny vessel has been transformed since they passed it in the blackness of space, freed of its antimatter trap and engine, its electromagnetic coils, its life support structures. It's just a bike now, more or less. The cyclist skids to a halt and stretches her arms over her head. She notices Lutetia, and the helmeted face nods a hello. Lutetia waves back, weakly.

Ultimately, the hike is an undeniable success. Iris got to bathe in the enormity of the cosmos and dance nearly weightless atop the highest point of the Belt's largest asteroid. Lutetia knows that the memories of Iris's awe and innocent wonder will be her companions forever, warming her against the coldness of time and comforting her in the recesses of age. Hektor is nothing but smiles, having fulfilled a dream he's had since Lutetia announced her pregnancy. At least, he's mostly smiles. That, and quite a few aches. As Hektor heads to the sauna to nurse his throbbing muscles and joints, Lutetia takes Iris to the mess hall for a snack and to let the inexhaustible wellspring of energy that is her daughter stretch her legs in an interior more spacious than the hab.

"Quite the view from Ahuna Mons, wasn't it?"

Leaning against the dessert counter, Lutetia spins her head to find a woman standing nearby, refreshing a cup of coffee. It's the cyclist.

"Yeah . . . yeah, it was something else," Lutetia stammers, surprised.

"Her first time?" The stranger gestures towards Iris, who is racing between windows and laughing as the view changes each time with the shifting of asteroids outside. Lutetia nods.

"Yes. And mine."

The stranger straightens up a little.

"Really? And what did you think?"

Lutetia glances at Iris.

"It was very special. How was your . . . ride?"

The stranger chuckles and looks at the pieces of her cycle disassembled on the workbench.

"Ever ridden a solar-cycle?" She asks. Lutetia shakes her head. The stranger pauses for a moment, and opens her mouth to say something when—

"Sylvia! There you are! We're ready for you."

Five women have just entered the mess hall, all with messy hair that bears the dishevelment characteristic of the combined effect of sweat and helmets. Sylvia waves them over.

"Who's your friend?" one of the newcomers asks, looking at Lutetia.

"Lutetia. Lutetia Vesta," Lutetia answers automatically.

"Lutetia, I'd like you to meet Juno, Doris, Daphne, Camilla, and Eugenia," Sylvia makes the introductions. Each woman waves in turn.

"Are you a cycling club?" Lutetia asks, a question that inspires a soft ring of chuckling to bubble around her. Lutetia's eyes dart between the women, unsure what she's said that's so funny.

"Not quite," Sylvia answers. "And who is this?"

"Irith!" Iris, having noticed her mother's lack of attention, has bounced over and is clutching onto Lutetia's leg, poorly feigning shyness as a grin breaks across her face.

"Hello Iris," Sylvia winks, then returns her attention to Lutetia as the other women swoon over the toddler. "We're not a club, to answer your question. These women are part of a loose community of deep-space, solo solar-cyclists. Some of them are so committed to it that they live this lifestyle full time as nomadic travelers. They all meet up regularly to gossip and support each other, but they're here now so I can interview them. I'm writing a book on their stories."

"Really?" Lutetia's eyebrows pop up and she glances at the other women, who smile and nod proudly. With a wave, Sylvia turns to walk off with these women, then pauses and looks back at Lutetia.

"Why don't you come with us?"

Lutetia is never able to fully explain why she accepts the invitation. Maybe it's the fact that she doesn't want to go back to their cramped hab, maybe it's that warmth with which the other woman had started playing with Iris, maybe it's something in the way Sylvia asked the question. Something in her tone of voice. Whatever the reason, Lutetia finds herself guided from the mess hall into the tunnels, emerging into a surprisingly spacious hall where a half-dozen women are already waiting. The chatter quiets as they observe Lutetia and Iris, but before long, the meeting is underway.

Sylvia has the room arranged into a circle, each woman pulling her chair into formation, all eager to watch Iris run around within this simple enclosure as she explores the new faces around her. At least the toddler is entertained. There are several minutes of laughter and light gossip during which Lutetia smiles and nods, and then, without any pomp or posturing, the women simply start to share their stories with the group.

They talk about their entry into the world of solo deep-space cycling, about the wonders they've seen and near tragedies they've survived. They talk about homes and families, or sometimes the lack thereof, the voluntary or involuntary reasons they turned to deep-space nomadism as a way of life. They share stories of treasured cycling routes and secret campsites, swap tips on fixing broken gears and engines and life-support units, and argue about which technologies will propel solar-cycling into the next generation. They exchange testimonies of what it is to be the only living being on a small asteroid deep in the Belt, soaring in enlightened isolation along the rings of Saturn, wondering at the limits of their own sanity during the long slogs between solid matter when nothing is visible save for the sparkling of inconceivably distant stars. Throughout all of this, Sylvia sits quietly, interjecting with only the occasional question as she transcribes their words.

"Those were some incredible women," Lutetia whispers, trying not to wake Iris, who has fallen asleep against her shoulder.

"That's why I do this," Sylvia taps on her tablet as the pair walk back through the tunnels towards Lutetia's hab.

"How'd you decide to write a book on women solo cyclists?" Lutetia asks, shifting Iris a little so she can talk. Sylvia chews the question for a minute.

"I was not in a good place when I discovered solar-cycling. The woman who introduced me to it, she helped me gain a sense of power over a life that seemed to be spinning out of control. She gave me clarity, she gave me an outlet, she gave me a community. It's not an overexaggeration to say that she saved my life. Remarkable woman. She used to talk about the speed of life in the age of space travel, how sub-light travel had made the solar system a little smaller, made us all a little closer. But in that rush to push our boundaries, we forgot the value of slowing down. To her, it was precisely the longer time commitment that cycling takes compared to standard space vessels that made it so invaluable. And she was right. Slowing down is what pulled me back from the brink. She died a few years ago, still leading seminars on solar-cycling and fighting the corporatization of space travel, still trying to keep a sense of community alive among cyclists. I wanted to do something to honor her legacy, so here I am. And here's you."

Lutetia blinks, then she realizes they are at the lift to her hab's airlock.

"Right," she shakes her head. "Thanks for today, Sylvia."

"Stop by again. And bring Iris, she's a treat."

Every day for the next week, Lutetia stops by the cycling group to chat with the women and learn more about their lives. Hektor is surprised at the sudden interest, but never contributes an opinion on the subject. He just smiles when she decides to go. Sure, he had planned a few more hikes for their time on Ceres, but he's still sore from summiting Ahuna Mons so he says he can use the time to catch up on some reading instead. He offers to watch Iris, but the other women have started to look forward to the toddler's bubbly presence.

At the meetings, Lutetia sits quietly in the background and listens with rapt attention as Sylvia conducts interview after interview, then mingles as the interview space melts seamlessly into a workshop, day after day. Tables and workstations are arranged, tools procured, more refreshments secured, and the cyclists set to work on tinkering with their bikes. A few of the women attract small congregations as they teach others how to reduce resistance in the spin on the electromagnets in the wheels, or how to optimize the antimatter reactions that produce thrust, powering the cycle through deep space. One group of women open a holo-schematic of the cycle's life support and habitation expansions that transform the vehicle into a sleeping pod. Sylvia guides Lutetia throughout the small clusters and groupings, sampling the knowledge and controversies and wisdoms circulating within the room. Before Lutetia knows it, she is seated on the floor around a pile of gears, helping them rummage through scrapped parts.

"So how did you get into solar-cycling, Camilla?" Lutetia asks the woman next to her, whose nose is millimeters away from a strand of coil quivering under close inspection.

"Needed space," she says simply. "Found it."

The other women in the circle laugh.

"Are you thinking about picking it up?" one of them asks Lutetia, who squirms a little as she feels her ears start to turn red.

"I don't know if I could," she admits. "I respect what you all do but something about the idea of solo travel has always made me uneasy, especially when you're talking about cycling through space. It seems lonely."

"I felt that way, at first," the woman says, a distant look in her eyes. "But isolation, when it's a choice, can be empowering. Most of our lives, we seek distractions so we're unprepared when there is nothing left between us and our own thoughts. Instead of hiding from that moment, I seek it out, confront it, explore it. I know what it is to interrogate my own mind."

Others around her nod quietly, each caught for a moment in their own recollections. Lutetia glances between them.

"Did you ever feel unsafe?"

Lutetia's timid question is met with guffaws and the rolling of eyes. She shrinks a little deeper into her collar.

"Why is it that people always assume a woman traveling alone should feel any more unsafe than any other travelers?" Camilla asks, waving the coil in her hands like a gavel. "All space travel is inherently dangerous, but we have ships that let us voyage with minimal risk and we train to use them. Tell me, Lutetia, did you fly to Ceres in a megaship?"

"No, just the family vessel," she admits. A few seats, life support, sub-light engine, ability to transform into sleeping quarters . . . all the same essential systems as the solar-cycles, only slightly larger and without using manual power to help charge the electromagnets.

"So, what's the difference?" Camilla snaps her fingers. "I've always felt I have more control in a smaller craft. More agility, more precision. And cycling keeps me in shape so I'm all sorts of buff. Nobody's messing with me when I arrive, I tell you that."

"We all have our reasons for solar-cycling," a woman named Ida turns to Lutetia as the others laugh along with Camilla. "I, for instance, value the ability to feel truly small in space, to connect with it by moving through it, and putting in the effort to do so."

"I used to bring my daughter cycling with me, when she was an infant," another woman chimes in. "It was precious, those moments spent together, drifting through space, determined to count every star in the sky as if it would stop her growing up. Now she's grown, and she still rides with me, in her own bike of course. But cycling to us has been something that we've shared across the span of a solar system."

Other women have noticed the conversation and migrate to the rummage circle, each sharing their perspectives and philosophies.

"It's a way to challenge myself."

"It's good for my health and the health of the solar system."

"I get to experience the universe for myself, just for myself."

"I just like being the boss," Camilla interjects, sticking her chin out proudly, then winks. "Without anyone calling me bossy."

The women laugh and cheer.

∽ • ∾

"Sad to say goodbye to Ceres?" Hektor asks Lutetia as she fidgets with the covers, head resting on his chest. She looks up at the stars through the skywindow in their hab, listens to Iris's soft breathing on the cot across from them. They only have a few days left on Ceres before heading to Pallas, the asteroid where they'll spend the remainder of their vacation.

"Hektor . . ." she says quietly. His left eyebrow pops up. Lutetia sits up to face him.

"I want to cycle to Pallas."

Hektor leans up on one elbow, confusion setting on his brow.

"You want . . . what?"

"One of the women said she can lend me a solar-cycle, and it's not that far of a journey. I checked the orbit charts."

"It's also not the easiest flight," Hektor chews his lip. "And you've never done it in a solar-cycle before. What brought this on? I thought you didn't care for cycling."

"That was before," Lutetia slumps back onto the cot. She runs a hand through her hair. "Before Sylvia, before the book, before meeting these incredible women and hearing their stories. I do so much with Iris, and I love it, but sometimes I wonder if I'm disappearing, Hektor. I need to try this. For me. You can follow me in the ship, I'll keep coms on the entire time, but I need to do this."

Hektor doesn't say anything for several seconds. Finally, he nods.

Lutetia spends several days practicing with a solar-cycle under the watchful tutelage of the cycling community. It's a smaller vessel than she's used to, but the controls are essentially the same. It responds effortlessly to every touch and command. The hardest thing to adjust to is the pedaling, but Sylvia says it's less taxing in deep space where the kinetic motion is just used to power the antimatter trap.

Finally, the day arrives for them to travel to Pallas. Lutetia helps load Iris into the family ship and hugs Hektor. He nods in a show of support, although his anxiety is written all over his face. Lutetia takes a deep breath and mounts her solar-cycle. It powers up, systems coming online, and she starts to pedal. Lutetia pumps her legs, leaning into the steering column, and then she engages the drive. The cycle vibrates only momentarily and starts to lift off the surface. Lutetia feels a whirl of excitement, heart pounding in her chest and nerves tingling. She's taken off from countless moons and asteroids in the family ship, but this is different. This is under her power. And before she knows it, Ceres is a sparkling gray sphere reflecting off her helmet. The hab structures and mess halls shrink as the asteroid falls away, and Lutetia turns her attention to the route ahead. In her rearview camera, she can see

Hektor guiding the family ship into position a respectful distance behind.

Lutetia switches the cycle to the deep-space drive and the engines hum. She pedals, feeling the magnets spin below her, amplifying her own kinetic energy and using it to snatch impossible particles from space and then exploding them to produce thrust. Through the asteroid belt she glides, feet pedaling now in a consistent, rhythmic motion, a meditation, a dance. Her heart relaxes and her thoughts calm, anxieties she was unaware she was even carrying dissipating into the black void of infinity. Around her is silence. Nothing but the gentle white noise of the engine, the pedals, her own breathing. White clusters of misshapen rock and ice swim in a pool of nothingness. The cycle swerves easily through the asteroid belt, a leaf on the solar winds, an air bubble on the current of space-time.

For Lutetia, the journey feels as if it lasts a lifetime. This has always been her home, her place in the universe, her existence. Although she knows the entire passage takes only a few hours to complete, she can hardly remember a life before the cycle. Everything else has melted away. She can't see any of her worries or anxieties in the void of space. They don't loom like the shadows of asteroids. They don't flare like the tails of passing comets. They are lost in the void, consumed by the nothingness. But what Lutetia *can* see through that nothingness is herself. For the first time in a long time, she sees herself. She sees clearly, sees herself whole and complete. She sees herself as a mother, as a wife, as a daughter, as a friend, as a worker, and as something more than just the sum of these parts. She sees those pieces of her life that had been buried under bills and work and the stress of keeping a family. They're still there, those pieces. Not lost, just hidden in the quiet of space. And she's found them.

By the time the in-helmet display starts blinking green and indicates the approach to Pallas, Lutetia has tears streaming down her cheeks. The asteroid grows and she navigates the field of debris surrounding it with relative ease, setting her bike on the surface with a soft thud and a stirring of sediment. Hektor lands the family ship behind her, and by the time he has opened the hatch, Lutetia is already upon him, leaping into an awkward embrace made more challenging by the space suits, and they topple slowly onto the ground, hovering a little in the miniscule gravity. She leans her helmet against his and sobs and giggles simultaneously. She wishes she could dry her eyes in this helmet.

"I take it the ride went well?" Hektor asks, sitting up. Lutetia laughs and nods, sniffling.

"Thank you, Hektor."

"What are you thanking me for? It was your idea. I'm glad it turned out to be everything you hoped."

"I'm sorry if I commandeered our trip with this cycling thing," Lutetia runs a hand over her helmet. "I know this was supposed to be about you taking Iris on the trip you did with your dad."

Hektor looked out into space, quiet for a moment.

"My dad loved coming out here because of the untamed wilderness of it. A chance to be a small part of a big universe. Off the beaten path. I may have taken Iris on the same trip, but you're the one who captured the spirit of it."

"Maybe we can pass that onto Iris," Lutetia says between sobs. "Like your dad."

Hektor squeezes her hand through the gloves.

"Like her mom."

"How was the ride?"

Lutetia and Hektor look up to see Sylvia's bike settling on the asteroid. She dismounts and bounces over towards them.

"Sylvia!" Lutetia squeaks. "What are you doing here?"

Sylvia smiles.

"You're a solar-cyclist now. Time to share your story."

She holds up the recording device and transcription tablet. Lutetia laughs, and nods.

THE LIBRARIAN'S FAMILIAR
∾ *Rose Strickman* ∾

The morning was already warm and sunny as Etta Hattrick poured aether powder into the tank of her velocipede, the granules hissing against one another. "There you are, Roger," she murmured. "That nice, now?" Her velly gleamed in response.

Behind her, the back door slammed. Etta looked up to see her mother—tall and gaunt, her gingham dress patched—pause on the doorstep, bucket dangling from her hand. "Going out again?" Agnes said. "Long route?" She coughed.

"Yes, Ma." Etta finished pouring in the aether. "Trotter's Loop."

Agnes hesitated. "I don't like you takin' that route, Etta. Long way, and that velly ain't safe." She shot Roger a disdainful glance and coughed again.

"Roger's safe enough." Etta set down the aether container, carefully screwing the lid back on and engaging the lock. "And someone's got to take the Loop."

"Don't see why it's got to be my daughter," Agnes sniffed. "But that's what you get for lettin' the government interfere, I s'pose. New Start!" She shook her head. "New Interferin', I call it."

"C'mon, Ma, Rosenfeldt's New Start Program's been good for us," said Etta. "I wouldn't have a job without it. We've been eatin' better since before Pa left, with the money I bring in. And you should see the people . . ." Her voice softened. "They just love the books I bring, Ma. Whether they can read them or not. It's like bringin' light to the darkness."

Well, she admitted to herself, not to everyone. Not to Tom McHenry, who lived along today's route. But she kept quiet about that.

Agnes gave another dry cough. "Bringin' light to darkness is the Creator's business, not yours, daughter. But all right: I guess

I can't stop you." She hesitated. "Don't s'pose you could read me one of them *Countrywoman* articles tonight?"

Etta hid a grin. Agnes might complain about government interference, but she was happy enough to have New Start library books read to her. "Sure thing, Ma." She checked the leather panniers on her velly, making sure all the books and magazines and scrapbooks were safely tucked in, along with her lunch. Then she draped on Pa's old leather jacket, cut down to her size, strapped on the quilted helmet, and slung a leg over Roger's saddle.

"Ain't right, that," Agnes grumbled. "Woman wearin' trousers. Flinging herself all over the place."

"Sorry, Ma, but we ain't allowed to wear skirts on our vellies. Might get caught in the wheels." Etta had her skirt bundled up around her waist, ready to be released when she dismounted her ride. She put her feet in the stirrups and began to pedal. Roger seemed to tremble with eagerness.

"Be careful now, daughter!" Agnes yelled as Etta and Roger headed out of the yard.

"Sure thing, Ma!" Etta shouted back, words whipped away by the summer wind.

∽ • ∽

Etta breathed a sigh of relief as she left the tiny farm behind. She might have lived there all her life, but as the years went by and the poverty that gripped her family and the country deepened, it had started to feel less like a home and more like a ruin. A ruin where she and her mother crouched, eating scraps, with Etta's father gone and her siblings a row of graves behind the house. Etta getting this job as a Velocipede Librarian had been a gift from the Creator.

Now Etta turned Roger away from the farm, away from the town nestled in the valley, climbing the mountain paths through the lush summer woods. Heat lay languorous over the mountains. Birds called out, squirrels scampered, and, despite everything, Etta relaxed. Roger's tires rumbled over the rough mountain path, handling its rocks and potholes easily, and Etta engaged the auxiliary aether engine as the terrain roughened and grew steeper. She gripped the handlebars and kept pedaling, enjoying the assistance provided by the aether tank. She grinned, enjoying the sense of freedom, control, and power her machine afforded her. Her velly was the first thing to ever give her a taste of such intoxicating feelings, and it was one reason why she loved her job.

"Good boy, Roger!" she called, and could almost convince herself that the machine responded, going faster, nearly leaping up the mountainside.

Etta ascended ever higher, legs pumping, aether engine vibrating, until she reached the first house on the Trotter's Loop route: a ramshackle cabin, tucked away in a hollow, moss dripping from its roof. Etta cut the engine and wheeled into the yard, paddling along with her feet, as a door slammed open and John Markson came running out, face alight with glee.

"Book Lady! Book Lady!" he called. "Hey, Ma, Book Lady's here!"

"I heard you." Mrs. Markson, face as lined as Ma's, came out, jiggling her new baby on her hip. "Hello there, Etta! You're a sight for sore eyes."

"Thanks, Mrs. Markson. Careful, John!" John was running his hands over her velly, eyes glowing with admiration. "This machine gets broken, I'll have to use a mule until we get it fixed." Which, considering how underfunded the library program was, might be never. She patted Roger reassuringly.

"Sorry, Book Lady." John backed up, still staring greedily at the velly. "It's just a beauty. I was readin' in that *Alchemy & Mechanics* magazine you brought—"

"Where's your manners?" Mrs. Markson whipped him upside the head. "Say good mornin'."

John gave a hurried greeting as Etta dismounted, then ran into the cabin to fetch the volumes Etta had left on her last visit. "How's your baby, Mrs. Markson?" Etta asked.

"Just fine." Mrs. Markson hoisted her daughter up, making her coo. "That *Countrywoman* magazine you brought had some good tips for makin' her sleep. Seems real good. Got any more?" She peered into Etta's panniers.

"Oh, yeah . . ." Etta began going through the books and magazines, even as John returned with the old loans. Mrs. Markson sighed with longing, and even John tore his gaze from the velocipede at the prospect of a copy of *Machinist's Companion*.

"I'm gonna do that," he said, peering at an illustration of the latest model of construction automaton from New Hanover City. "I'm gonna go to the city and make 'tons for all the rich folks."

Etta sighed at the thought of such a future. "Sounds lovely, John. You should do it."

"Really?" John looked up, eyes shining with hope and hero worship.

"Absolutely. Soon as you're sixteen, you can get a job with New Start. Just think: you makin' it big in New Hanover." Etta gave an elaborate bow. "Mr. Markson, machinist!"

"Wow, Book Lady . . ." Still starry-eyed, John wandered off with his new issue of *Machinist's Companion*.

Mrs. Markson bit her lip, watching him. "You shouldn't encourage him, Etta," she said quietly. "There ain't no money to send him. And lots of folks . . . they don't like all this government interference, New Start and all that."

Etta sighed. "I know, Mrs. Markson, but without New Start, I wouldn't have a job. Ma and me'd be starving."

"Exactly." Mrs. Markson nodded, holding her baby close. "Some folks say you and the other Velocipede Librarians have sold out to the government. Or worse."

"Worse?" Etta's ears pricked.

"Folks like the Holy Mountains congregation. Say aether's stuff from Shaitan and you librarians is rollin' in it. Sayin' you got sin on you, workin' for the government. So be careful, Etta. I'd hate seein' anything bad happenin' to you, or the other librarians."

Touched, Etta smiled at her. "I appreciate it, Mrs. Markson, but we'll be fine. Sheriff Jamison's made it an offense to hurt or dishonor a Velocipede Librarian. He had the last offender whipped in public before jailin' him, remember?"

Mrs. Markson just shook her head. "Be careful, Etta. There's folks along this very mountain who'd like to see you come to harm."

∽ • ∾

"Hold your courage, Roger," Etta murmured as they approached a particular hollow further up the mountain. "We're comin' up on the McHenry place."

She wheeled Roger in, slow and quiet. Under her hands, Roger seemed to growl, as though it liked this place no more than she.

The McHenrys lived in a miserable little hollow high up the mountainside: dark and gloomy, with a sullen stream running beside it, flowing down toward Suttley Creek. Etta peered around, searching the shadows. Perhaps it was due to her conversation with Mrs. Markson, but she was feeling even more nervous about approaching the McHenrys than usual. With any luck, Lucy would be home and Tom would not—

Roger must have hit a hidden root or stump; the velocipede suddenly fell over sideways, dragging her along with it somehow, her clothes all tangled in its pedals. Etta found herself tangled up in her own velly, lying sideways on the leaf-strewn ground, as the gunshot cracked above her head and the bullet whizzed by.

"Shaitan's whore!" A bow-legged man in a tattered hat, skin caked with grime, came striding around the cabin, gun held to his shoulder.

Fear gave Etta strength. She scrambled to her feet, pulling Roger with her. "Beggin' your pardon, Mr. McHenry, but I ain't no whore." She prayed her voice didn't tremble. "Just a Velocipede Librarian, here to bring you and your wife some books—"

"Shaitan's books." Tom McHenry took up a stance between Etta and his cabin, gun still ready. He spat a long stream onto the ground. "Got nothin' but darkness and filth in 'em. *Government* books. I told my wife she ain't gonna read no more of them. And you'll stay off my property, witch!"

"I ain't no witch, Mr. McHenry." Etta backed up a step, holding Roger between herself and Tom. "Just a librarian—"

"You're peddlin' them devil government books." Tom squinted at the velly. "And I see you, witch. You're one of them that the aether likes."

Etta would have been exasperated if she wasn't so terrified. "Mr. McHenry, aether's a natural substance. It don't come from Shaitan."

"Ain't natural stuff." Tom gave another spit. "Won't have it on my property." He glared at her. "And you've got its marks all over you, witch. Its power's in you, and in that Shaitan-made machine of yours." He tapped his cheekbone. "I've got the Sight, same as my grandma. And I Sees you. You've got the power of the aether in you. Get along, and take that Shaitan-cursed machine with you!"

Slowly, Etta began to back up, wheeling Roger. "I'm gonna have to report you, Mr. McHenry," she warned. "Sheriff Jamison's made it an offense to threaten a Velocipede Librarian."

Tom's only response was to jerk his gun at her. Etta kept backing up, Roger still growling under her hands, until they reached the main trail again and she could finally let herself tremble.

$\sim$ • $\sim$

"Oh, Roger." Etta, midway through her nightly cleaning of Roger, leaned against her velly's framework. The warmth and solidity of the shed enclosed her, reassuring. "What a day."

She shivered at the memory of Tom McHenry and his threats. "Creator-bless, that was scary. I'll report him next time as I'm in town, but . . . I hope he don't do anything too bad in return. How're we going to get Lucy her books?" The McHenrys were so poor they never even came into town. And Mrs. McHenry lived for the books Etta brought.

In the light of the kerosene lamp, Rapid Roger gleamed, its engine shining as Etta oiled and polished. The velly seemed to purr under Etta's ministrations, leaning close like a cat. Etta laughed at her own fancy. "Ah, you're a good velly, Roger," she said. And it was. The velocipede's wheels gleamed like silver, every spoke shining and cared for.

Etta looked at Roger fondly. John was right, she decided: her velocipede was a wonderful machine. The New Start's velocipede drives had reaped a surprisingly ample harvest, and engineers and machinists employed by the program had done amazing work fitting out the donated vellies with auxiliary aether-powered tanks. The librarian program wouldn't have been possible without the augmented machines. "How can even Tom McHenry think you come from Shaitan? And what was he talking about, the aether likes me? Its power's in me?" She laughed. "Foolishness. If I had the power of aether in me, I'd be long gone." She smiled at the image. "Just think of it, Roger. You and me on the road, leavin' all this behind. Going across the whole of Atlantis. Maybe even taking one of them airships across the sea."

Roger hummed with pleasure at the thought. Etta laughed again shaking her head. "Etta, you're dreamin' things," she said to herself, and began putting the rags and oil away, taking up the lantern to head back to the house, and Agnes. Still, she couldn't help adding, "Good night, Roger."

Roger gleamed its own good night while Etta swung the shed door shut and locked her velocipede in.

Etta didn't expect to see either of the McHenrys until next week at the earliest, when she took the Trotter's Loop route again. She was thus surprised to encounter Lucy McHenry a mere two days later.

She and Roger were cycling along the Suttley Creek route, shorter and less steep than Trotter's Loop, but still deep into the mountains. True to its name, the trail ran alongside Suttley Creek for most of the way, and the running water babbled happily, flashing among the rocks. The late-summer birds sang among the full-leafed trees, and the squirrels chattered as Roger zipped along the trail.

Etta was thinking about Tom McHenry as they drove along. She'd invented excuses not to go to town to report him—the farm, Agnes and her cough, the library routes—but she knew it was simple cowardice keeping her from the sheriff's office. The memory of Tom's blazing pale eyes, the gleam of his gun, kept her awake at night. Was it true, what he'd said about having the Sight? And if so, what did he See?

It was almost as though Roger spotted Lucy first. The gears locked in place, and Etta found she could no longer pedal. "Roger!" Etta scolded, and broke off when the woman in the berry patch jerked her head up, eyes wide. "Oh. Hello, Mrs. McHenry," she said, feeling foolish.

Lucy McHenry jerked her head in nervous acknowledgement. As might be expected of Tom's wife, she was a pale-faced, rail-thin woman, wearing an old, patched dress and an old-fashioned sunbonnet, her expression habitually nervous. She carried a twig basket, half-filled with berries. "Good afternoon, Book Lady."

"I didn't see you at your place the other day." Etta dismounted Roger and wheeled it over. "Are things all right?" She didn't quite want to describe her alarming encounter with Tom to his wife.

"Oh, things are . . ." Lucy trailed off, not looking at Etta. "Are those more books?" Her eyes fastened hungrily on the panniers.

Etta hesitated. "Mrs. McHenry . . . I'm not sure . . . your husband . . ."

"Oh, please!" Lucy stared at her, eyes pleading.

Etta gave in. "All right, take a look. . . ." Etta unloaded the volumes and spread them out for Lucy's inspection. Lucy sighed, tracing her fingers over an old issue of *Countrywoman*.

"You know I don't read so good," she whispered. "But I'm so much better since I started borrowing your books, Book Lady. I practice all the time. And I love them pictures." She looked up, eyes shining. "Do you think them ladies in New Hanover City really look that elegant all the time?"

"I'm sure they do." Etta drew herself up, trying to imagine her threadbare hand-me-downs were silken couture like she'd seen in the newspaper fashion plates. Lucy held herself straighter, as though imagining the same.

Etta sighed, putting away the fantasy. "Here, why don't I read to you right here? I got time, and it's a lovely day." And Tom McHenry was nowhere nearby.

"Well . . . guess it can't hurt. . . ." Lucy hovered, torn between longing and anxiety. "Just for a spell."

Etta leaned Roger against a stump, where it glowed content in the sun. "Which would you like, Mrs. McHenry?"

Lucy asked for a serial adventure story in *The Reader's Companion*, and listened rapt as Etta read aloud, the sun a warm glow around them, the forest ringing with birdsong.

When Etta finished the story, Lucy sighed. "Thank you, Book Lady. That was beautiful." She hesitated. "What do you think will happen, now their ship is wrecked?"

"Well, I've got the next issue in here." Etta dug it out. "Maybe we can read it together sometime, when you're away from home."

Lucy sighed with longing. "I'd love to take it home, Book Lady. But Tom would have himself a fit. He said—" She broke off.

"Said what?" Etta asked when the silence stretched too long.

"He said them books were Shaitan-made," Lucy whispered. "And you've got the power of Shaitan in you, Book Lady. He says aether and aether machines is cursed from Sheol."

A loud, angry metallic twang rang out. Both women jumped and looked at Roger, leaning against the stump, a spoke still vibrating. The sun gleams on the metal had taken a new, furious edge.

Lucy lowered her voice and stepped closer, as though the velly might hear and take offense. "He says that thing . . . he says your velly's half alive. He says the power of aether's gotten in you and you've given power back to your machine. He says you're a witch and that's your familiar."

Etta couldn't help it: she burst out laughing. "Oh, Creator-bless, Mrs. McHenry, what'll he say next?"

"Ain't no laughing matter." Lucy shook her head. "I bring a book home, or he sees you on the property, I don't know what he'll do." Still, her eyes lingered with unnerving hunger on the next issue of *The Reader's Companion*.

Etta sighed. "All right, Mrs. McHenry. I understand." She started to put the magazine away.

"Wait!" Lucy cried, making Etta freeze. The older woman licked her lips. "Listen . . . why don't I take that back home and hide it?"

"You sure about that?" Etta's eyes widened. "Mr. McHenry—"

"He don't have to know." Lucy spoke rapidly, eyes still gleaming with that deep hunger. "I'll hide it and leave it in the hollow tree down the way from your place when I'm done."

"I don't know, Mrs. McHenry. . . ." Still, Etta found herself holding the magazine out. Lucy snatched it and held it close to her heart. Etta sighed. "Just make sure Mr. McHenry don't find out," she said in a low voice.

Lucy's eyes shone. "Thank you, Book Lady."

⟆ • ⟅

Etta thought about the encounter all the rest of the day and came to a decision. The time for cowardice was past. If Lucy was that desperate for books, despite her husband's opposition, then the situation was dire. Tomorrow she would go report Tom McHenry to Sheriff Jamison, gun or no gun. But that night, Agnes took sick.

Etta awoke to horrible hacking coughs, echoing up to the loft where she slept. Disoriented and still half asleep, she staggered down the ladder to find Agnes thrashing on her bed, body lashed and convulsed by the force of her coughs. Etta spent all night caring for her, brewing a honey tea by lantern light and placing hot compresses on her chest, but Agnes kept coughing until dawn.

"Etta . . . sweetheart . . ." Agnes rasped. The morning light revealed no blood spots on the counterpane, to Etta's inexpressible relief, but Agnes was gray-faced and exhausted.

"Hush, Ma. Just rest." Etta hurried about. It was clouding up outside: great heavy black clouds. They were in for a bad rainstorm. "I got to get to town, get the doctor, before the rain hits—"

The first scud of rain hit the window just as Agnes coughed again, so bad she fell out of bed. As Etta helped her back, the rain increased and she realized there would be no going to town today, not for any reason: not only would the rain wash out the dirt road, but Agnes clearly could not be left alone.

The rain continued, hard and pounding, for three days. Etta ran between chores and her mother's sickbed, too busy even to think about going on her library routes. She barely found time to maintain Roger.

"Oh, Roger," she whispered, soft and miserable, when she did snatch a minute. The rain pounded on the roof of the shed. "I'm so worried about Ma . . . her cough's gettin' a little better—I think—but she needs a doctor. . . ."

Roger hummed a little in sympathy. Etta smiled at the notion as she set aside a piece of the engine she had disassembled for cleaning.

"Sometimes I wish you *were* alive," she murmured. "Alive and could understand me . . . you'd want to help, wouldn't you?"

Roger gave a gleam of agreement. Etta began assembling the engine again. "Well, we'll get back on the road soon as possible.

Get to town, get the doctor." She grimaced. "And tell them at the library depot what's been happening here that I can't go on my routes. And report McHenry to the sheriff." She sighed. Just a few days ago, life had been simple. Now there were far too many complications.

She replaced the reassembled engine and patted Roger on the saddle. "Thanks, Roger. You're a good velly."

It was just her imagination of course, but she thought she felt her velly purr, solid and reassuring.

∽ • ∽

That afternoon the rain finally stopped. The next day dawned, if not exactly clear, then with flashes of sun peeping from the scudding clouds, shining on the rain puddles. Agnes lay collapsed in bed, still coughing now and then.

"Creator-bless, this is foolish," she whispered as Etta fed her soup. "Bein' so sick—" She broke off in another volley of coughs.

"Hush, Ma. And it ain't foolish to be sick. I'll go to town, soon as the road dries a little, and get the doctor."

Agnes gave a rasping sigh. "Darlin', I'm not sure you should be wastin' money on a doctor. Everyone's got their time."

"No!" Horror seized Etta. "Don't talk that way, Ma. Don't jinx yourself. You'll get better!"

Agnes just sighed again and coughed.

Etta waited until that afternoon, when the road had dried enough for Roger's tires, to wheel the velly out. Her conveyance buzzed with urgency and anticipation under her hands. "Ready to run, ain't you, Roger?" Etta couldn't help smiling. "Well, let's hurry!"

They zipped down the hillside toward town, Roger dodging every puddle, seeming to choose the fastest, driest path along the soaked, rutted road, as eager as Etta. Nearby, Etta could hear the thunder of Suttley Creek, and when the road wound near the creek, she saw the waters risen high and gray, sweeping fast as racehorses down the mountainside. "That storm really did a number," Etta murmured to Roger, and yelped when the velly suddenly halted.

"Dagnabbit, Roger—!" Etta's curse was broken off when she saw the colorful, sodden square of paper on the roadside. Dismounting Roger, she picked her way through the mud to inspect it.

It was an issue of *The Reader's Companion*. The very same issue she'd given Lucy just before the storm.

The scenario flashed through Etta's stunned mind like a reel from one of those new moving pictures: Lucy hiding the magazine, but not well enough. Or maybe she got bored during the days of heavy rain and brought it out. Tom seeing. Tom yelling, ripping it from her hand. Tom throwing the journal out the door, to be washed down the mountainside. Tom grabbing his gun, vowing to his cringing wife that he would get the Shaitan-cursed Book Lady this time—

There came a loud *twang* of metallic alarm from Roger. Etta looked at her velly, one of its spokes still vibrating with urgency. And she looked up the slope, toward the farm, where her mother was lying sick and helpless. . . .

Etta was never sure, afterward, exactly what happened next. There was just a blur of motion, of frantic strength, then she was mounted on Roger, engaging the engine recklessly, screaming "Go! Go! Go!" as they raced back up the road, the wind whipping through Etta's hair.

It happened just before they would have arrived at the farm.

Roger's handlebars—*twisted*. Etta felt them move. They twisted of their own volition, and Roger turned, running off the road into the woods.

"Roger! Stop!" But Roger kept tearing through the trees, wet leaves spraying up from its tires, engine whistling, and Etta was helpless to do anything but hold on.

Roger came to a halt by Suttley Creek, rushing strong and violent between its banks. Etta dismounted Roger and pushed it aside, falling into the leaf litter. She staggered, panting—then screamed when she saw what was happening in the water.

There was Tom McHenry, waist-deep in the racing creek. In his huge hands, gasping and twisting with terror, was Agnes, her clothes and hair soaked and streaming in the current.

"Stop!" Etta barely recognized the voice tearing from her throat. "Let her go!"

Tom looked up with a savage smile. "I came huntin' you, witch," he snarled. "But you wasn't there. Only your ma. Ain't no crime to drown a witch, nor yet a witch's mother. . . ." And he thrust Agnes's head down again. She plunged with a scream, limbs splashing in the water.

Etta was hardly aware of the sudden metallic shriek behind her, the movement as Roger stood up on its wheels. She only knew that she was sliding down the steep clay bank, into the freezing water, the velocipede just behind her, and then she and Roger both were lunging at Tom, Roger's engine snarling.

"Witch! Witch!" Tom, white-faced, struck at the animated velocipede as Roger charged him, growling, water spraying up from its churning wheels. In the confusion of Roger's attack, Tom let Agnes go. Etta lunged, grabbing her insensible, half-drowned mother under the armpits and hauling her to shore. She pushed Agnes up the bank, as high as she could, before turning back to the battle.

Roger was rearing back and striking again and again, handlebars and front wheel smacking into Tom, engine glowing white with aethereal power. "Witch—Shaitan—Sheol—" Tom gasped, fending off the velocipede's attacks.

Etta stood stock-still, the icy current pulling at her. She felt her own rage, animating Roger, and she felt the aether, powering its engine. How it *shone*, how it flowed and wove in such intricate patterns, and how easily it could be plucked from those patterns, how easily it could be bent to her will—

Flames leapt from Roger's engine, an arc of aether-white light, onto the flailing Tom. Tom howled as the aethereal fire spread, flames biting into his flesh, chewing, eager. He broke away, flailing, head and back a bonfire, and flung himself headlong into the deepest, fastest current in the creek.

Etta and Roger watched while Tom McHenry was swept away, the flames still burning even beneath the water, a dim white star in the darkness of the creek, devouring even as the water grasped the man, holding him down, surging away. He did not surface again.

Etta's knees trembled. She collapsed, falling with a splash. The creek churned around her waist. She could barely breathe. What had she done? What had she done?

A whizzing splash. Roger appeared at Etta's side, nudging her like a cat eager for praise. She patted his saddle unthinking. "Yes, Roger, very good. Thank you. . . ." The velocipede purred with pride and pleasure.

Bracing herself on Roger's saddle, Etta hauled herself back to her feet. Together, she and Roger headed back to shore, Roger's wheels spraying water, to where Agnes still sprawled on the bank, unconscious. "Help me?" Etta said, and draped Agnes's limp form over Roger's saddle. The velocipede wheeled up the bank, Etta climbing alongside, holding Agnes safe.

Once they made it to the top, Etta took one breath, then another. The wet chill was catching up to her, penetrating her numb shock. She thought back over the events of the last few minutes, but they didn't make any sense, even in her own head.

Roger churred in impatient inquiry, nudging her with a handlebar. *Can we go home now?*

Etta reached out to pat its saddle. "Yes. Let's go."

Slowly, the velocipede rumbled out of the woods, Etta walking beside it, holding her unconscious mother in place.

Images reeled through her mind: the abandoned magazine, Tom holding her mother under the water, Roger charging through the creek. The aether fire burning underwater, eating Tom's flesh. The realization that Tom was right: Etta was a witch, of a kind she did not understand.

But for now, she could not regret anything. For now, she was simply deeply glad that she and her mother were alive and that they were in the company of Etta's miraculous, gallant, aethereal *familiar*.

GOBLIN SUPERMARKET
∽ Elly Blue ∾

*I*mportantly *victorious, Clamor, Avenger of Shadows rose roaring from the battlefield.*

I stare at the blinking cursor on my screen. Do I fix the commas? Cut the adverb? Cut the whole paragraph? Kill this terrible story episode deader than Clamor's cartoonish enemies?

I decide to go for a bike ride to clear my head. And get a sandwich.

Wheels whirring, muscles working, I navigate traffic lights, cars, dog walkers, potholes, puddles. My senses alert, I'm grateful for the realness of the world I inhabit when I'm not churning out content for the NightLands serialized fiction app.

Someone's behind me in the bike lane, so I stand on the pedals to give myself more power coming out of a red light. Sure, I get a little competitive. There aren't a lot of parts of my life where I feel like a winner, but here on the road I love the virtuoso feeling of balance and speed, bike and body working together. I peek in my handlebar mirror and glimpse an upright posture and the kind of derpy bike that usually has a couple kids on the back. I refocus on the road ahead and let some thoughts about Clamor the Avenger's upcoming adventures creep into my mind. It's time for a sex scene, according to the NightLands formula. Maybe Clamor will take a wounded enemy from the battlefield as a hostage, but it'll be a really sexy enemy with a surface wound on his broad chest that needs to be carefully cleaned and bandaged. . . .

Whoosh! I nearly topple as a collection of shapes and colors materializes beside me in the lane, far too close. Regaining my balance, I see the mom-bike I thought I'd left in my dust a block ago pulling ahead with the telltale whir of an electric assist.

"Cheater!" I grumble at the retreating ponytail.

She's not moving as fast as I'd thought and turns to look just as I flip her the bird. Her eyebrows go up and her hand does too in an exaggerated wave as she clumsily shifts gears and zooms off, pedaling hard and getting far too much forward momentum out of the effort. The rage swells in me for a moment, and then I see the tiny, kid-size helmet strapped to the empty child seat on the back. That brings me right back down, feeling like enough of an asshole that I don't bother trying to catch up. This is low blood sugar in action, I tell myself. It was a good call to break for lunch. I take the final ten blocks easy, waving cars past me at stop signs, aggressively looking to not pick a fight.

Because my life is a bad joke, she's there, locking up at the sole rack outside PDX Veg. There's already one bike on the rack, and she's struggling to maneuver her giant, stupid SUV of a bike into a position where her U-lock will fit around both the staple and her bike's tank-like frame. I sigh loudly, then make a big production of locking my trusty steel-frame ten-speed to the fence around the restaurant's recycling bins. Part of me is rolling my eyes hard at myself, another part is genuinely annoyed by this poseur, and a third is just thinking about the sandwich I'm about to order and the cookie I'm going to inhale while I wait for it.

As I click my lock shut, I realize the electric bike woman isn't going into the shop. She's standing there looking nervous, with a hand resting on her bike seat. She clears her throat and says, "I'm sorry I passed you too closely back there."

I'm so surprised that I reflexively say, "It's fine." Then I remember that I'm working on being less passive-aggressive and add, "It was a little close and I was surprised, but no harm was done, and I shouldn't have flipped you off. That was rude, I'm sorry."

She smiles a little, but it looks more like a grimace. She gestures at the bike. "I'm still figuring this out. It was my 40th-birthday present to myself, and I haven't been on a bike since college."

"So it's not just like riding a bike?" I say wickedly, and she lets out a little laugh that's a bit more genuine.

"I don't know," she says. "It's so fun, though. At least when it's just me on the road. Whenever a car or another bike comes along, I realize how rusty I am."

She seems nice, and I don't want to say anything disparaging about her unfortunate choice of ride, so I open the restaurant door and gesture for her to go in. "Thanks," she says, but when we get to the counter she waves me ahead of her. "I have a big order," she says. "You go ahead." I could hug her for that, but instead I order the seitan salad sandwich with extra Vegenaise and a chocolate chip cookie. The cookie is warm in my hand as I sit in an empty booth and focus on devouring it. My job is goofy as hell, but I do get caught up in it and forget to eat. I'll have to figure out a way to get Clamor hooked up with some baked goods. Sweet rolls could be a thing in his world. Maybe he goes to a village bakery to quench his hunger post-battle, and the baker's assistant is a buxom babe who invites him to warm up by the oven. . . .

The mom cyclist appears at my table. "Do you mind if I join you?"

I wave to the seat across from me, chewing the last of the cookie. I'm feeling better already.

"So how did you decide on the bike for your 40th?" I ask. I'm still embarrassed about my road rage and don't particularly want to talk about myself, so this seems easiest.

"Oh, well, uh." She gives a little stammer and is clearly trying to figure out what version of her story to tell. "I've been working at home for the last couple years, like most people, and I wanted to give myself a reason to get out more. Expand my world. Help out with my niece. And I don't know if I'm just out of shape or it's long Covid or what, but I just don't have a ton of energy anymore, and I get out of breath really fast, so the electric bike seemed like a good idea. And I just had a sort of windfall." She stops, looking flustered, like she hadn't quite meant to tell that long of a version of the story. "I'm a writer, and my book had a good quarter for sales." She ends sounding both like she's apologizing for something and like she's regretting saying so much, and then shrugs. "So it all just sort of worked out. I really love the bike, though. It's been a while since I had this much fun."

"You're a writer?" I'm fully alert now, the sugar from the cookie hitting my bloodstream.

"Yes, mostly I do copywriting. For, like, plumbing supply companies and that sort of thing. But I've been writing fantasy stories too."

"So was your windfall from the plumbing or the fantasy writing?"

She laughs again, and I warm to hear it. "It was just a fun little fantasy novella I put together. Like, a really light, low-stakes story. I wrote it for my sibling when they were postpartum and having a hard time, and my friend published it, and I expected like twenty people to ever read it. But that was right when COVID hit, and I guess everyone wanted a cozy fantasy because it went viral. A major publisher picked it up, and then I could afford this bike. And, like, rent. And fancy groceries for a few months. Toys for my niece."

"Wait," I say. "Wait. Are you the author of . . . *Goblin Supermarket*?"

She grins and ducks her head. "Yup, that's me. I really don't know where it came from. Or if I can ever do it again." She spreads her hands.

I'm just staring open-mouthed, so shocked that I barely notice my sandwich getting plunked down in front of me on a plastic tray.

"I don't know where to start," I say. "That book really helped me get through those early days. The way Derina tries so hard to get in trouble, and the people around them just lowkey look out for them." She's blushing, so, hero that I am, I tone things down by going negative. "But why was it print-only at first? That was annoying, I read the first two chapters online and got totally hooked, and then I had to wait for it to come in the mail." Real smooth.

"Oh, my friend doesn't believe in e-books," she says. "It's a sustainability thing, I guess the servers use more energy than we think. Did I mention that her publishing company is *tiny*? But her theory is that the book sold so well because it couldn't be easily pirated at first, at least until Tower picked it up. I don't know. I have a complicated relationship with technology, to be honest. Let me show you. . . ." She digs in her purse and my jaw drops again when she pulls out a flip phone. "I'm just at the computer all day writing, and I know if I had a smartphone I would never put it down."

I'm still speechless and there's a bit of a pause. "What about you?" she asks. "You look like you never fell off the wagon with bicycling." Then she looks flustered again. "I didn't mean, I mean you do look very fit, but—"

"It's okay, I know what you meant," I say with a grin, blushing a little myself. "The bike's my therapy, my transportation, my best friend, everything. I don't know what I'd do without it. I'm . . ." I hesitate, feeling foolish, but forge on. "I write for a living too. Fantasy too, but it's for an app called NightLands. It's more like ghostwriting, my pen name is on the books, but it's all written to formula and people subscribe to read it serially, and I get paid based on how many people read it, so that really drives what I write."

She perks up. "I've heard of these apps. I'm actually really interested in this."

"Julie!" calls a voice from the other room. "Oh, it's my sandwiches," she says. "Listen, I need to get back to my sibling's place with these, but I'd love to learn more about your work. It's always nice to meet a colleague. I'm sorry again about earlier."

"Me too, let's forget it happened." I pull out my smartphone, open up a new contact page, and hand it to her. "I'd be happy to tell you about NightLands, but honestly, you can do so much better."

"Maybe." She chews on her lip while she focuses on putting her info into my phone. I notice myself staring and look away.

After she leaves, I dig into my sandwich, feeling starstruck and off-balance. Julie Marwan. Who the hell knew.

Her book really is something special, and I try to pick apart why. A misfit goblin teen getting a job bagging groceries is not the most compelling premise, but its strength is it gives you the kind of feeling you never want to end. That's the emotional response that the NightLands formula is aiming at, but even though her book isn't perfectly paced, I didn't care because it worked on another level. The goblin runaway, Derina, makes questionable choices on every page, and they still find meaningful connections and a sense of belonging. It's a far cry from the sort of crap I write, where good-looking, self-centered adults win every fight and reap the rewards. I flash back to myself flipping Julie off on her bike and cringe again.

Back home at my desk, I press and hold the delete button for a while. Text melts away under my cursor, and it's satisfying to watch Clamor's misdeeds and sexploits disappear into blank space. I stop deleting right before the episode's opening fight scene, when Clamor is thundering through the forest to seek righteous revenge.

Clamor's fury was interrupted by a small sound coming from the bushes. He wouldn't normally stop, but there was something familiar about that sound. Something that sapped the battle tide right out of him, replacing it with a sharp burst of memory of being very small and very young. He pushed aside a branch and found not a child but a ragged adult, hunched over and sobbing.

When I stop for the night, far later than usual, Clamor has missed all of his plot points. He has skipped the big battle, de-escalated a tavern brawl, and protected a petty criminal from being arrested by the King's army. He has had zero sex scenes, though a smoldering look and a tender kiss have been bestowed upon him, promising more to come for the voracious NightLands readers. I'll write that spicy bit in the morning after I, he, and the kind-eyed but surprisingly sharp-tongued Vala, whom he comforted in the forest and is now helping to find her missing stepbrother, have all had a good sleep. I have a feeling that the stepbrother might be the real love interest, but I'll save that awkward realization for tomorrow, too.

By lunchtime the next day, the episode is ready to post. I put a content note at the beginning for Clamor's regular readers: *unexpected character development, clumsy attempts at emotional maturity, warriors sheathing their swords.* Let them make of that what they will. I hit "submit" on what feels like the final salvo of a vainglorious career and get my bike out. A sandwich would hit the spot, and I've earned two cookies this time around.

I find myself expecting to hear an electric bike the whole way there, and the restaurant feels weirdly unfamiliar. I get out my phone, planning to start looking for new jobs, but find myself pulling up Julie's contact info. She entered her full name—no hiding behind a pseudonym for her!—and a number with an area code I don't recognize. I hesitate with my thumb over the message icon, then scroll down idly and see with an electric twinge that she's added a note: *I hope you call me :)* I hadn't ever noticed there was a field like that.

I send her a text: *Sandwiches this weekend?*

Then I check my NightLands analytics. There've already been a couple dozen opens for the new episode. There hasn't really been time for any reviews, but as I'm looking, I see a notification pop up: a four-star rating. It's the opposite of what I expected, and while I stare at it, another notification obscures it, this one with five stars. Then, just as I'm starting to feel my lungs expand again, a one-star review comes in with a comment: "WTF is this? WokeLands?"

I expel a too-loud bark of laughter, drawing a look from the couple at the next table. A four-star review pops up. Then another five. Wow.

I've got to tell Julie, I think, and check my messages again. Nothing. My heart sinks.

Then I remember what it used to be like to text on a flip phone and, taking a deep breath for courage, hit the call icon.

She answers on the first ring. "Hello, it's you, right? The bicyclist? From PDX Veg? I hoped you'd get in touch, but then I worried a little too much about it because I didn't get your name."

"My name's Liz," I say, putting her words in a special compartment in my foolish head to obsess over later. "Uh, I'm actually here now and realized I should have called you before heading out. But what are you doing Saturday?"

"I'm babysitting Saturday, but is it too late to join you right now? I just hit a wall with the plumbing blog."

"Absolutely. What's your order? I'll get it in the works."

"Okay, but you are forbidden from paying for me."

Of course, I pay for her vegan pastrami sandwich and iced tea, not being a complete dolt. While I wait to order, ten more ratings come in: another one-star, a two-star, and the rest fours and fives. "Cozy Clamor???? I'm here for it," one of the fives adds.

The most absurd plot point is that I might still have a job after all.

When Julie arrives, we just grin awkwardly at each other for a long beat, and then we're both talking at once. I tell her all jumbled together about Clamor's new direction and how her book made me feel, and she tells me that she's opened up her drafts folder for the first time in months and absolutely can't talk about her new idea but it makes her feel the way the last one did and that's a good sign, isn't it?

I think it's all a good sign. After lunch, we walk out together, and our shoulders brush electrically. Our bikes are parked together on the rack, handlebars and seats snugged together. She stops abruptly on my bike's side and turns toward it, breathtakingly close. "Maybe I could ride a bike like this again," she says. "I was thinking about it, and that's the whole point of gears, right? They help you get up the hill? I wouldn't mind trying." She turns her face up to look at me, glowing.

"I was actually going to ask to test-ride your bike," I say, which is technically true since I thought up the idea several fractions of a second ago. "I'm a judgmental prick about bikes, but I hear people ride these to expand their worlds. I could use a bit of that."

That's how I end up on an electric assist bicycle for the first time. It's neither as motorized nor as painfully dorky as I expected. In fact, I appreciate the way the upright posture and low center of gravity give me the freedom to look around and enjoy the delighted determination on my companion's face as she steers my trusty steel steed with barely a wobble.

I insist that we ride to her house so I can drop her off. She insists that I come in.

Readers, you deserve a happy ending as much as either of us does, but you'll have to wait for the next episode to find out for sure.

CONTRIBUTORS

Avery Vanderlyle is a Boston-based writer of sci-fi, fantasy, erotica, and romance—sometimes all at once. Her work has appeared as part of Circlet Press's online Halloween microfiction series of erotic SFF stories, and in the charity anthology *His Magical Pet*, among other places. She's on Mastodon at https://mastodon.social/@AveryV and blogs infrequently at https://averyvanderlyle.wordpress.com/.

Cara Brezina is a freelance writer who lives in Chicago, Illinois and loves biking on the Lakefront Trail. In addition to sci-fi and fantasy stories, she writes educational nonfiction books on a wide range of topics.

Christopher R. Muscato is an adjunct instructor and writer from Colorado, and the former writer-in-residence for the High Plains Library District. He has published over a dozen short stories, including ones in *Shoreline of Infinity*, *Solarpunk Magazine*, and *House of Zolo*, and is better at writing about bicycles than riding them.

Elly Blue manages day-to-day operations at Microcosm and rides an electric bike around Portland with her dog.

Jamie Perrault is a queer nonbinary veterinarian and writer from the American Midwest. They are mother to delightful twins, and married to a wonderful genderqueer spouse. When not reading or writing, they can be found playing the clarinet, hiking, and watching tokusatsu shows. Feel free to find them online @ awritinghope on Twitter or at their website jamieperrault.com.

Lisa Timpf is a retired HR and communications professional who lives in Simcoe, Ontario. Lisa's speculative fiction has appeared in *New Myths*, *Third Flatiron*, *Acceptance: Stories at the Centre of Us*, and other venues. Her speculative haibun collection, *In Days to Come*, is available from Hiraeth Publishing. You can learn more about Lisa's writing at lisatimpf.blogspot.com.

Kathleen Jowitt writes fiction across many genres exploring themes of identity, redemption, integrity, and politics. She lives in Ely, works in London, and writes on the train. Find her at kathleenjowitt.com and follow her @KathleenJowitt.

Rose Strickman is a fantasy, sci-fi and horror writer living in Seattle, Washington. Her work has appeared in anthologies such as *Clockwork Dragons*, *Robotica*, and *Sword and Sorceress 32*, as well as online e-zines such as *Luna Station Quarterly* and *Aurora Wolf*. She has also self-published several novellas on Amazon at amazon.com/author/rosestrickman.

Shelby Schwieterman is a writer, performer, and day-job worker living in Los Angeles, California. You can see them play video games at https://www.twitch.tv/r2shelby2 or listen to their voice on *The Rom Complex* and *Formulaic* wherever you like to find podcasts.

Taru Luojola is a Finnish polyglot writer and translator, known to be reading never-heard-of books in odd languages all the time. They've written and published several velopunk novels and short stories in Finnish and English.